Samuel Clossy

Observations on Some of the Diseases of the Parts of the Human

Body

chiefly taken from the dissections of morbid bodies

Samuel Clossy

Observations on Some of the Diseases of the Parts of the Human Body
chiefly taken from the dissections of morbid bodies

ISBN/EAN: 9783337255367

Printed in Europe, USA, Canada, Australia, Japan

Cover: Foto ©Andreas Hilbeck / pixelio.de

More available books at **www.hansebooks.com**

OBSERVATIONS

On some of the

DISEASES

Of the Parts of the

HUMAN BODY.

Chiefly taken from the Dissections of MOR-
BID BODIES.

By SAMUEL CLOSSY, M. D.

LONDON:

Printed for G. KEARSLY, in Ludgate-street.
MDCCLXIII.

PREFACE.

KNOWLEDGE being the perception of the agreement or difagreement of Ideas, that knowledge is more compleat by how much more thofe Ideas are conformable to the Types they are taken from. But Ideas are either General or Particular: and general Ideas being formed of particular Ideas; by leaving out the difference, and preferving the reft, particular Ideas are more conformable to their objects than general Ideas, and knowledge drawn from particular Ideas more exact than knowledge taken from general Ideas; and our knowledge of Subftances and their affections acquired from particular Ideas more exact than fuch knowledge from Ideas made general by abftracting. Perfect it cannot be, forafmuch as our Ideas of Subftances with the nominal comprehend not the real effence of the object; therefore from the nature of the human mind, and its operations and powers, there can be no uni-

verfal

verfal propofitions made about fuch fubjects admitting unexceptionable proof.

Now as all human knowledge is derived at firft from fenfation, and improved and enlarged by the operations of reafon and reflection, fo our knowledge of the affections of the Human Syftem is acquired by feeing the fymptoms and diffecting Bodies, and both are improved by reafon and reflection.

We muft therefore commence with obfervations and experiments, and draw general conclufions therefrom by the method of induction : It is true indeed the arguing from experiments and obfervations by induction is by no means fufficient for general conclufions ; yet it is the beft way the nature of the fubject will admit of, and may be held as fo much the ftronger, by how much the induction is more general ; by this means we proceed from effects to their caufes, and from particular caufes to more general ones, till the argument end in the moft general ; then we affume thefe caufes fo difcovered, and by them explain the phænomena of the fymptoms, and prove the explanations ; and this is the method which I have endeavoured to follow in thefe obfervations, where examples of the fame kind would admit.

By

By the word Difeafe, I underftand fuch an affection of the whole animal fyftem wherein the functions of its feveral parts are difturbed, or fuch an affection of any part that difturbs its function; and fo a fever is fuch an affection of the whole fyftem, wherein the functions of its feveral parts are difturbed; and a jaundice fuch an affection of the Liver as difturbs its function.

By the word Symptom I underftand a preternatural affection refulting from a Difeafe, either of the whole fyftem or any part thereof; fo the heat in a fever, or the high-coloured Urine in the jaundice, are preternatural affections refulting from the difeafes of the fever and jaundice.

The caufes of difeafes are whatever produces the difeafes, and may be termed either material or immaterial; of the immaterial caufes are the paffions of the mind, which may either difturb the uniform motion of the whole fyftem, or any part thereof. A fudden fright has fufpended, and even totally ftopped the motion of the whole fyftem; and the paffion of fhame has diffufed the Blood through the Neck and Face. Of the material caufes are the febrile matter, which being in the Blood

a 3   raifes

raises the fever, whether it be by irritation, or obstruction, or an institution of nature to depurate the Blood ; and **the acrid** or inspissated Bile are causes material of the jaundice.

But causes also are either antecedent or immediate ; of the antecedent are the Air, Diet, Exercise, Secretions, Sleep, and Passions of the Mind; **all which,** by preternatural quality, quantity, or motion, may introduce affections preternatural in the Fibres **or Fluids, which** are causes immediate.

Immediate material causes are discoverable either by reason or dissection; and so when a sudden profuse hæmorrhage cures that sort of blindness termed gutta serena, we infer that the cause of the blindness was a swelling of the Retina, whereby the medullary Fibres of the Tunic suffered compression by intumescence of the Vessels; and a tumor or water compressing the optick Nerve within the Skull, or a wasting of the Nerve, is found to be the cause of the same sort of blindness, not by reason, but dissection. The investigation of causes by meer reason is, I believe, what comes under the denomination of Theory or Ætiology of diseases, and is rather to be held as the most easy and intelligible manner of conceiving how

how fymptoms are produced, than what the caufes really are.

While I was endeavouring to trace fuch caufes of difeafes, as can be difcovered by dif-fection, in St. George's hofpital in London, and Stevens's hofpital in Dublin, by the invi-tation and permiffion of the late Dr. Stevens, in the years 1752, 1753, 1754, 1755, 1756, and keeping an exact regifter thereof; together their antecedents at the time, with fuch re-flections as the phænomena feemed to me to fuggeft, I thought I obferved fome things lightly paffed over by authors, and others where their experience was defective. The fyftems are furely of exceeding ufe, as they fhew us what to look for in due order and method ; and indeed Galen himfelf fays, we ought to have fome plan of univerfal theorems, and exercife ourfelves in particular examples * ; yet the concifenefs to be obferved in drawing up fy-ftems will fcarce admit of fuch diffufive de-fcription as the importance of the fubject re-quires, or as is fufficient to convey exact ideas.

But in all this attendence I had no opportu-nity of feeing what might be the caufe of the

---

* De meth. medend. lib. 9.

　　　　　　fympsymptoms of sense, intellectual powers, and motion, when the causes are such as can be objected to the senses ; and being at a loss about these things, Mr. Butler of Stevens's permitted me to see if among his patients, wounded in the Head, if I could find any thing relating to the subject. Now in those observations though I did not succeed to my desire, for among other defects I did not see what symptoms followed from the Cerebellum in being compressed, broken, or otherwise affected, yet as what I there saw may carry with it some degree of illustration of the affections of the Head, arising from internal causes, and be useful to the younger surgeons, I have drawn them together, agreeable to the plan laid down in some other of these sections, which, with the rest of the cases, should the reasoning be erroneous, may serve in part those whose taste for such subjects may incline them, and leisure afford opportunity, to draw up more elaborate systems.

For while I was thinking over, and duly digesting, what I had observed of some other affections, whose causes are gathered from reasoning chiefly, and going on observing at Mercer's, finding myself under a necessity of intermitting these disquisitions, and probably for a considerable time, I have chosen the following,

ing, as of more general ufe, till freedom of thought, and a more eafy fituation, fhall afford **time** and power to proceed on fo defirous a bufinefs.

It is true indeed our knowledge of fuch caufes as are found by diffections, is not of fuch general ufe as of thofe objected to imagination and reafon chiefly ; for all epidemick and intercurrent Fevers, Fluxions of different fpecies, and Hyfterical difeafes, come under this head, **which are by much** the greater **part** of the fubjects under the care of Phyficians ; yet they are not to be rejected becaufe they are incurable ; for, by our intelligence herein, we leave the fick, whom we cannot reftore, **no worfe** than we find him ; **nay** it is **even** more than this, for there is fcarce any difeafe of the parts, or even of **the** whole fyftem, that will not admit of fome **relief,** which every humane man will endeavour to adminifter ; but we are alfo inftructed in the confequences of difeafes whofe progrefs and effects might be checked when incipient.

I faid above, fhould the reafoning be erroneous ; for though I am certain that a free communication with the external air is by no means effential to the formation of Pus ; the Pus in the

upper

upper and lower Venter, (in the former of which
I have seen it where there has not even been
a fiffure of the Skull evident to fenfe; and in
the latter I have feen it in the **very** center of the
Liver, where there could not be fufpected even
the leaft impurity depofited from the Blood into
the part which might inflame it) is an inconteftible
proof of this propofition; and I have likewife feen
it deep in the Mufcles of the Loins and Thighs,
where the external caufes which gave origin to
it did not even break the Skin.

But that pure Blood, extravafated without
communication with the external air, fhould
put on fuch a modification of parts, whereby
it may come under the denomination of Pus,
I cannot fay that I am fo exactly fettled in : for
having advifed with very good judges among
the furgeons while I was reviewing thefe obfervations, and whofe experience in thefe mat-
ters is more extenfive than mine, I find they
are inclined to think that it is rather the refult of
an inflammation; though at the fame time they
do not affirm the impoffibility of the change.
Now fince the fettling of this propofition does
not feem to interfere with the practice, we
fhall let it lie over, till common general experience, (which with reafonable men will always

7   be

be the ſtandard of truth in theſe ſubjects) ſhall approve or reject it.

I ſhould probably make ſome apology for the too liberal uſe of the word Sleep. Sleep in due reſtriction is ſuch an affection of the whole man, as is inſervient to refection and nutrition, being an inſtitution of nature to that end; whereas the train of ſymptoms ariſing by compreſſion, or other ill diſpoſition of the Brain, is by mechanical affection; but I have uſed the word to convey the whole company of ſymptoms, by exciting the idea of ſleep; nay, truly, for endeavouring to illuſtrate or prove propoſitions by ſo few facts as have fallen within my experience, excluſive of the narrowneſs of my genius in drawing deductions, were I not afraid of Cato the ſenior's cenſure, *Recte quidem, mi domine vir, ſi modò Amphyctionum decreto conſtrictus evulgas hæc.*

C O N-

CONTENTS.

SECT. I.

Of the HEAD.

SECT.

CONTENTS.

SECT. II.

Of the NECK and CHEST.

SECT. III

Of the LIVER.

SECT. IV.

Of the DROPSY.

OBS.

CONTENTS.

OBS.

CONTENTS.

OBSER-

OBSERVATIONS

ON

DIFFERENT DISEASES.

SECT. I.

Of the HEAD.

OBSERVATION I.

Lethargy and Paralyſis from contuſed Integuments.

IN ſummer **1752**, a young woman was brought to Steevens's, who received a ſtroke with a ſkellet on the left Parietal Bone, bruiſing the Integuments twelve days before. The whole Head was ſwelled, and together with the Neck covered with an eruption like that in the meaſles in the two or

A   three

three firſt days of that diſeaſe. She could not ſtand erect, but if left to herſelf, would reel, and tumble, and ſleep. In the place of contuſion two ſections were made, at right angles to each other down to the bone; and the angles being raiſed and removed, no fracture could be traced. The wound was ſuffered to bleed and ſuppurate; in ſome days it digeſted and healed, and ſhe perfectly recovered.

If from an external violent cauſe, therefore, a Drowſineſs and Paralytick affection ariſe, attended with an Eryſipelas over the Head and Neck ; we may ſometimes conceive the former rather as proceeding from a compreſſing of the Brain, by being overcharged from the obſtruction of the external Membranes of the Head, than as ſymptoms of preſſure from extravaſation in the internal Membranes, and eſpecially if no traces of fracture appear to the ſcalper. This eryſipelatous appearance has been obſerved by Henry Francis le Dran *, a man of great circumſpection, ſagacity, and experience, who aſſigns it to the wound of the Membrane of the Skull, or other aponeurotick expanſion, and that it may be held as a ſymptom of violence done to theſe Membranes.

* Obſ 15. and Operations, London, 1749. 370.

O B-

OBSERVATION II.

Lethargy from Extravasation on the
Dura Mater.

In April **1752**, was brought to
Steevens's a man about forty. Eighteen
days before he was thrown by a horse
against a wall that struck him oblique
on the left Parietal Bone. The Integuments being lightly contufed, he was
fomewhere dreffed fuperficially, and
thought to be fecure. The feventeenth
day from the accident, the day before he
came to the hofpital, he grew drowfy,
and a general refolution of the whole fyftem of the Mufcles fucceeded. The
eighteenth day he flept profoundly, and
fnored without fenfe or voluntary motion; the Integuments being raifed, no
fracture appeared. It was determined
however by the Surgeons to trepan
him; which being accordingly done, as
foon as the piece in the crown of the
Trephine was removed, and even before, the matter flowed out, and continued to difcharge from between the
Dura Mater and Skull. In the evening
he awaked, and the matter being all dif-

A 2 charged,

charged in a few days, he recovered both his underſtanding and motion.

Blood extravaſated, therefore, will put on the form of Matter, that is to ſay, it will corrupt without contact with the external air; and if it increaſes in quantity, will, by its preſſure only on the Brain, incommode the functions of the Organ: For as the Dura Mater, by the experiments of Haller *, is deſtitute of feeling and motion by irritation in common with the Membranes of the two inferior Venters, it could not be that the want of ſenſe and motion in the whole ſyſtem did ariſe from the quality of the extravaſated and ſtagnant fluid, acting on the Membrane, but did by its preſſure only ſtop the propagation of that which being communicated to the Fibres of the Muſcles, puts them into motion, and to the Fibres of the interior parts communicates motion, which from habit is not attended to by the *thinking thing that is within us*; and Blood may be extravaſated many days on the Dura Mater without any damage to the Membrane. The ſafety therefore of deferring the Trephine, as in the preceding, may be indubitably ſettled, for it would have been uſeleſs there, though the ſymptoms were the ſame.

OBSERVATION III.

Lethargy from Extravaſation between the Membranes.

The 25th of October 1755, a boy of fourteen, on the left ſide of the head,

* On Irritability, &c. p. 18. Lond. 1755.

received

received a kick from a horfe which cut up the Integuments to the very bone. He lay for fome time quite motionlefs; when he came to himfelf they conduct- ed him to fome place where he was dreffed fimply, and feemed tolerably well to the feventh of November, when he became drowfy and ftupid, and was brought to Steevens's, being thirteen days from the accident. The day fol- lowing he fell into a deep fleep, and his right arm became quite paralytick. The Integuments being removed no fracture appeared, but being trepanned on both fides of the Coronal Suture, from the Foramen in the Frontal Bone came out an inconfiderable quantity of Pus, and from the Parietal Foramen nothing. The next day he flept deeper than be- fore, and his Pulfe was quick and de- preffed. On the fixteenth day from the accident his **Face was** inflated, his ftools and urine came off **involuntarily**. The Dura Mater being cut through in both Foramina, fome Pus came up from the Pia Mater. In the evening of this day he died.

A 3

The

The day after the Integuments of the whole Skull being removed, the tendon of the Frontal Muſcles with the Pericranium appeared quite ſeparated from the Bone down to the orbits of the Eyes. The Skull being ſawed and raiſed with as much of the Dura Mater as lined it, the Pia Mater and Brain were exhibited to view. A ſmall effuſion of Pus was ſpread ſuperficially on the Pia Mater, and ſome Blood Veſſels paſſing to the longitudinal Sinus divided, and the Membrane every where thickened. On removing the Membrane and ſeparating the Hemiſpheres, ſome part of the Pus was obſerved covering the Corpus Calloſum, yet the Brain did not ſeem injured in its organical conſtitution. Now the Dura Mater being removed from the part of the Skull ſawed off, there appeared near the holes of the Trephine a fiſſure of the Inner Table which croſſed the Suture, paſſing obliquely to the External Table, ſcarce diſcernable to the eye, and without any injury perceptible to the External Table: nor was there any

Pus

Pus or Blood between the Dura Mater
and Bone.

The application of the Trephine, therefore, is not
fo likely to fucceed, if the extravafation is between
the Membranes as if above the Dura Mater only;
for Blood and Pus may diffufe themfelves too far
on the Pia Mater to be emitted by trepanning; and
if the Veffels on the Pia Mater bleed below the Membrane, the Blood may fall between the Hemifpheres,
and there corrupting deftroy the Brain. Now from
the fmall quantity of the expanded matter, which
could make but a flight impreffion, having fo much
fpace for its expanfion, it is probable the Brain fuffered in its organical ftructure, fo that its medullary texture was broken like jelly in a glafs, tho' the
change, as not tranfparent, was not evident to fenfe,
for the fiffure internal fignified the Impetus of the
Vibration, communicated by the Pulfe of the Cranium, was loft in the Brain; which has been likewife obferved by the judicious Monf. le Dran *.

O B S E R V A T I O N IV.

*Lethargy from Extravafation below
the Pia Mater, and among the Membranes.*

A man about thirty, on the fecond
of March 1755, received a ftroke with

---

* Obf. 17. Lond. 1740.

a pole on the left Parietal Bone, which fractured the Skull to splinters, and wounded the Membrane. On the eighth he was brought to Steevens's: the wound being cleansed and the splinters removed, the Trephine was applied on the 12th, being drowsy, indolent, pale and dispirited. When the piece, taken out by the Trephine, was examined, the Inner Table appeared separate from the external: the motion of the Dura Mater was strong in the hole; the lethargy continued. On the fifteenth the Dura Mater was cut through, but no Blood issued from beneath. On the seventeenth in the morning he died.

The Cranium being removed, Pus was expanded on the Dura Mater around the hole of the Trephine, to the breadth of the palm of one's hand, and the Dura Mater being removed, an equal surface of Pus was diffused on the Pia Mater. Now at one place under the stroke and the fracture, the Pia Mater appeared black, and on slitting

the

the Membrane a clot of Blood was difcovered which had formed for itfelf a cavity
in the fubftance of the Brain, as large as
a pullet's egg, but not corrupted.

Blood, therefore, extravafated from the Pia
Matter, may not only diffufe itfelf fo far as to fall
between the Hemifpheres, but force its way into
the fubftance of the Brain, and there accumulate.

OBSERVATION V.

Lethargy from a Depreffion of the Skull
and Corruption of the Brain.

A man about 40, on the fourth
of April 1755, had a portion of the
Frontal Bone, on the left fide, depreffed with the ftroke of a fpade,
which depreffion was fhaped like a
notch.   On the fixth he was brought
to Steevens's. The feventh and eighth
he was ftupid and drowfy with frequent convulfions.   On the ninth he
raved.   The Trephine being applied,
the depreffed part raifed and fplinters
of the Inner Table removed, Pus and
Blood came from beneath the Bone:
To the 16th of the month he continued in a deep fleep without convulfions;
and

and being the twelfth from the injury, he had tremors and sweats, and
then died.

The Cranium being removed, the
Membranes were lacerated and the
Brain, of the size of a cubic inch,
was corrupt underneath.

Convulsions may be therefore caused by the
splinters of the Internal Table pricking the Brain,
and may sometimes indicate the existence of splinters
pointing toward and piercing the part; for by the experiments of the celebrated Haller, the Membranes
are constituted void of sense or perceptive powers; and
in the preceding, where the Membranes were divided
to search for extravasated Blood or Pus, I observed
neither expression of pain, or motion such as arises
from irritation without pain; though the want of
either sense or motion in these cases, is by no means
an argument of their want of either in a state of
health; for the Brain is so affected in all wounds of
the Head, that probably it may not convey to the
mind the idea of continuity solving in its Membranes at those times.

OBSERVATION VI.

*Lethargy and Paralysis from a Con-
cussion with Extravasation.*

A very fat man about forty (coachman to commissioner Burke) on the
tenth

tenth of May 1755, fell down back-
ward in the ftable under a coach horfe;
the horfe, frighted and ftarting, fet his
foot on the man's head at the left fide of
the Frontal bone, and rammed it to the
ground; the Integuments being lightly
bruifed, he was treated in the country
as if only contufed, yet he was not fo
well but they fent him to Steevens's on the
21ft, being the eleventh day from the
accident; he fevered flightly in the evening with horrors and thirft, but in
two hours the fever intermitted, and
returned in like manner on the 22d,
23d and 24th; then a flight Paralyfis of the left Thigh fucceeded, and
when about to fit down he plumped
into the chair, as if a Paralyfis of the
whole fyftem of Mufcles had caufed
it. On the 25th he was drowfy, the
lower Mandible convulfed. On the
26th, he raved: the Trephine was
applied immediately under the bruifed Integuments; Pus appeared in the
Diploe, a little on the Dura Mater,
and a fmall quantity came up from
the Pia Mater, when the Dura Mater
was

was cut through. The Lethargy per-
fisted. On the 28th of the Month,
and the eighteenth day from the accident in the evening he died.

When the Integuments were removing the following day, the Pus
appeared every where expanded on
the Frontal Bone under the Pericranium, which was shaken from the
Bone. The Cranium removed, exhibited the whole surface of the Dura
Mater, on the left side, covered
with Pus. The Dura Mater, being
cut and removed, shewed the Pia
Mater in like manner overspread ; and
in the part of the Skull which remained on the Spine, diametrically opposite to the hole of the Trephine, between the Membranes, a considerable
quantity of clotted Blood was accumulated and flatted by their pressure ;
but the Skull itself, either in the part
sawed off or that which remained
on the Spine, was no where injured.

Hence we may see how strong the vibration of
the Shell is sometimes from a return of the stroke,
so as to be able to shake off the Pericranium and

Dura

Dura Mater on both fides the Bone, for it is by the
ftrength and quicknefs of the Vibration, that this
feparation is effected, and that the veffels between
the Bone and Membrane, and between the Membranes, being divided, the Blood diftils, from
whence the Pus, overfpreading the Membranes,
arifes; and from hence we may likewife deduce
how dangerous a fign it is, when a drowfinefs and
Paralyfis continues after dividing the Membranes,
and the Skull is no where injured, or but flightly
fiffured, as in Obf. III.

Moreover in a concuffion with extravafation, the
extravafation may happen on the fide oppofite to that
where the ftroke is firft given. Now as the Paralyfis
of the left thigh was firft obferved, being the fame on
which the Head received the firft fhock, we may fay
fometimes that if the Paralyfis be of the fame fide with
the contufion, an extravafation is on the oppofite; for
the Paralyfis of the left thigh was firft obferved and
more evident, and the clot, by whofe preffure it was
caufed, much thicker than the fuperficies of Pus on
the left fide; which to my knowledge hath not hitherto been obferved; not indeed is the obfervation of
any great ufe; for the ftrength of the Pulfes of the
Skull going and returning, has very probably fo
fhaken the Brain, that its medullary tracts preferve not
that pofition and diftance among themfelves which
may be fervient to the due functions of the Organ;
nay even were it otherwife, that the Brain preferved
its Organical ftructure, yet as there is no indubitable
mark for the Trephine to fix on, the letting out the
Matter or Blood is thereby impracticable, even were
it between the Dura Mater and Bone.

O B.

OBSERVATION VII.

Lethargy from the Brain, broken and putrified.

In July 1752, came a youth about eighteen to Steevens's, who had fallen from a horse perpendicularly fourteen days before ; and from the time of the fall he was drowfy, filent and inert; he rarely opened his eyelids, and when he did, the Eyes feemed quite motionlefs, the bruifed Integuments removed, no fracture appeared. The Trephine being applied on the Crown, near the Sagittal Suture, no Blood came from the Membane nor Pus ; the Membrane being cut through, nothing came from beneath ; the Lethargy continued. On the third from his arrival, and the 17th from the fall, he convulfed. On the 18th he died lethargick.

When the Cranium and Membranes were removed, among which there was no Pus or extravafated Blood, the Brain was found broken at its bafe, and

and putrified, but without extravafated Blood about it ; or in the Membranes near it.

The fuddenneſs and continuance, then, of the ſymptoms of the ſame tenor, and their degree, may ſometimes ſignify a rupture in the Brain, and it alſo appears,
that a drowſineſs may ariſe from the Brain being
broken without preſſure by extravaſation : So the effect of the Pulſe of the Shell, returning by the Impetus on the oppoſite ſide, may not only ſeparate the
Membranes from the Bone and extravaſate Blood
thereby, but the very Brain itſelf may be likewiſe
broken : The Impetus was firſt received on the
Crown, and the Baſe of the Skull, returning the Vibration, effected this rupture by ſuddenly propagating its additional Momentum through it.

Nor, from all the foregoing caſes, can it be determined on what day the drowſineſs will ſucceed
from the fall, or other impulſe ; for in Obſervation
the ſecond, it came on the 17th ; in the third, on
the 13th ; in the fourth, on the tenth ; in the fifth,
on the 3d ; in the ſixth, on the 15th, and in the
ſeventh, on the 1ſt ; it being according to the effect
of the impulſe, or intenſity of the preſſure, the
Brain receives from the extravaſation, or rupture.

OBSERVATION VIII.

Lethargy with Fungous Excreſcences.

In November 1753, a boy about ten
years old was brought to St. George's
in

in London, who received a blow with a pole in Hyde-park that fractured the Skull: In some days after he was trepanned on both sides the Sagittal Suture, (the fracture crossing the Suture) and the Membranes cut thro'. Now the Brain puffed out of the Foramina to an inch or more at every dressing, and was constantly cut away, and thus continued till he died. He slept likewise with an obscure delirium the whole time.

It should seem, then, as if the Brain had a motion independent of its Membranes, as all organical and animated parts have: for it could hardly be the motion of the Pia Mater, which is so weak a Membrane, that by repeated Systole did express this Fungus; and for the Dura Mater from its adherence to the Skull at the Sutures, and in the intermediate spaces by vessels passing between the Bone and Membrane, it seems totally incapable of Systole. And in all the foregoing cases, the visible motion of the Dura Mater did not seem to be the motion of the Membrane only, but of something whose impulse to the finger was stronger than the motion of the Membrane could be; which you will readily perceive by passing your finger through the hole of the Trephine, and pressing the Membrane firmly.

But

But herein I do not confider the caufe of its motion, whether it arife from a fwelling of the Cortex in expiration, or exifts in the part as an Organ in action, independant of the motion of the Heart.

Moreover whether thefe excrefcences of the Brain correfpond in proportion to a fuppuration in other foft parts, to which Monf. le Dran * feems to compare them, or whether owing to the mere inteftine motion or agitation of the part, I do not affirm. I once faw an inflamed tefticle which abfceded, fhoot out a fungus in a manner not very diffimilar. Now if it is the nature of Glandular Bodies abfceding fo to do, it may be fome fort of argument that the Brain is of the Glandular kind.

OBSERVATION IX.

Epilepfy from the Dura Mater ab-
fceding.

In the year 1752, a man about 30 was brought to Steevens's, who had epileptick fits returning feveral times a day for three years. On examining the Head, there appeared a fulnefs on the left Parietal bone, which had remained from a ftroke of a faplin about the time of the commencement of the fits.

* Obf. 24. Lond. 1740.

B   The

The Integuments being raifed, it was difcovered to be a fwelling in the Bone; the Trephine being applied in the place, in the operation the Bone was found cellulous and fpungy with Pus in the midft ; to the Bone the Dura Mater firmly adhered. In fome Days after he died in a Lethargy.

The Cranium with the Dura Mater being removed, there was a circular afperity on the infide the Bone, about the fize of a crown, and feveral abfceffes in the Membrane about the fize of peas adjacent to the hole.

A Bone therefore may fuffer by contufion an extravafation in its Diploe. The extravafated Blood, by corrupting, may effect an abfcefs in the Bone, as in the foft parts when fo affected : which corrupted Matter will foften and fwell the Bone, and produce the difeafe termed by the Arabians * Spina Ventofa ; probably as the Bone in this difeafe feems inflated, and being obferved oftener in the Spine than other Bones, this was made an univerfal Name for fuch Diftemper in any Bone. If this difeafe happens to a Bone of the Head, an inflammation may be raifed in the Membrane underneath, which terminating in one or more apoftems, may induce an in-

* Avicenna, lib. 4. Fen. 4. Trac. 4. Cap. 8.

curable

curable Epilepfy, a drowfinefs and death; and this
may rather be occafioned by the Pus or Ichor of thefe
apoftems, or by the vapour expiring toward the
Brain, and thereby difturbing it, than any fpafm
of the Membranes, for the reafons laid down in the
preceding; which have been alfo noted by the noble
Hungarian Kovats Tatai *: Becaufe, when the
Brain is irritated with fharp Matter, the whole animal falls into convulfions; and the Pia Mater, being connected by Veffels to the longitudinal Sinus,
and in the intermediate fpaces by veffels between the
Dura Mater and it, and its want of irritation and
fenfe, is equally incapable of fpafms, held fometimes
as caufes of the fits.

We may likewife note what ferious attention an
extravafation in, or a diftemper of, the Bones of the
Head merits, and how ufeful the Trephine turned,
till you get to the midft of the Bone, may be, when
early applied in fuch affections: for thus you let out
the extravafated Blood, Matter or Ichor, which
otherwife will foak through the Inner Table to the
Membrane. A fimilar cafe you will find in the Obfervations of Le Dran †.

In the obfervations related, we have feen apoplectick fymptoms arife from extravafations of Blood
and Pus between the Dura Mater and fkull, as in
the fecond; between the Membranes, as in the third
and fixth; from the extravafated Blood forcing into
the medullary fubftance of the Brain, as in the fourth;
and that paralytick fymptoms arife from the fame

* De Epilepfia Ultratrajecti 1670.   † Obf. 27.

caufes; and that they are all fatal unlefs the Blood has an exit, and the Brain and its Membranes are free from permanent impreffions, as we have feen in the fecond cafe. Whereby we conclude how ufeful and juft thofe rules of the Surgeons are, when they repeatedly and diffufively bleed in all wounds and concuffions of the Head, to prevent thofe fatal effufions, and abforb that which may have extravafated while fluid, before it can run into clots by ftagnation. And in all thefe we may remark that where the Brain is the part affected, the powers of the underftanding are likewife affected; which may lead us fometimes into the part precifely affected in paralytick diforders, as they have their caufes exiftent in the Brain, **Medulla Oblongata,** or Spine.

And that fimilar extravafations happen from internal caufes, as when the veffels are eroded by fharp Lymph flowing in their Tunics, tranfudation from rare veffels, or rupture from plenitude, we have the authority of the Royal Society to prove. For Cole * tells us, that an hyfterical lady, who had been liable to Hæmorrhages of the Nofe, on a neglect of bleeding, her ufual remedy, and an ill-timed ufe of Aftringents, was taken with a violent pain in her Head and a faultering fpeech, and fo died immediately. On opening the Head next day, he found the veffels in the Membranes of the Brain, the Pia Mater efpecially, on the right fide of the Head, being the part fhe complained of, turgid with Blood, and the Membranes being cut, emitted from

* Tranf. Phil. vol. 3. 29.

beneath

beneath a great quantity of bloody Lymph, and in the substance of the Brain an ounce and half of grumous Blood, which had formed for itself a cavity. The famous Anatomist Marcellus Malpighius, as we are told by Lancisius, being seized with a Vertigo, a loss of speech, a contortion of the Mouth, and palsy of the right side, was taken off with an apoplexy. In the right Ventricle of the Brain were found near two ounces of extravasated Blood, with more than half as much of yellow Phlegm in the left Ventricle. And * Adams found in the left Ventricle of a woman, who died of an apoplexy, near five ounces of clotted Blood, the whole right side of the Trunk and extremities being first seized with the palsy.

Moreover that the same symptoms may sometimes arise from the Serum or Lymph sweating from the Membranes, and by its pressure, whether it exist among the Membranes or in the Ventricles, hindering the due function of the organ, or the propagation of the Will along the medullary tracts to the Fibres of the Muscles or interior nervous Membranes or parts, we have the authority of Wepfer † to depend on, who was one of the most learned and ingenious Physicians of those times: He tells us that Jacob Reutinger, a full man, about fifty, and given to excesses, some weeks before he died had so violent a pain in his Head that he was quite distracted; about three weeks before he died he became totally blind, made urine involuntarily, grew paralytick, first in his right and then in his left Leg; at length

---

* Transf. Phil. vol. 5. 210. † Obf. 1 de Apop. Scaphusi, 1675.

fell

fell down in a violent apoplexy, in which continuing four days he expired. On raiſing the Skull and wounding the Dura Mater, the water jetted up, leaving a more than natural ſpace between the Membranes; the like was obſerved between the Pia Mater and Brain ; the Brain had imbibed it plentifully ; all the Ventricles were full, even the canal of the Spine itſelf. And that Urſula Frigen, in her 37th year, and during her being with child, had violent pains in her Head with a Vertigo ; in her fourth month ſhe fell down in a violent fit of apoplexy, deſtitute of ſenſe and voluntary motion, in which ſhe continued three days, then ſenſibly came to herſelf, except that her right Leg and Arm remained paralytick, and her Underſtanding weakened : In her nine month ſhe became melancholy ; and from the time of her lying-in, till her 40th year, continued unequally ſo, and died of a pleuriſy : On removing the Skull, the Dura Mater ſeemed raiſed up as if by vapour, its Arteries turgid ; under the Pia Mater all parts were immerſed and ſoaked in Lymph ; the Ventricles full ; the veſſels of this Membrane turgid ; Lymph round the Medulla Oblongata ; and ſome too flowed out of the Spine ; in the right Plexus Choroides ſeveral Hydatids, of which ſome were larger than a pea ; in the left Ventricle there were likewiſe ſeveral, one of which was greater than an hazel nut ; the Cerebellum flaccid ; the Spinal Marrow ſmaller by much than it ought. And * Conradus Bruner tells us that Chriſtopher

* Obſerv. Celebrium. Amſterdam, 1724.

Weiler,

Weiler, in his 64th year, an inceffant drinker, a
fmith by trade, fell down dead in an apoplexy, as
he was at dinner in his fhop; the whole fpace
between the Membranes was filled with Serum; all
the veffels and cavities, even the fourth Ventricle,
and the whole Bafe of the Skull were inundated, together with the Canal of the Spine, in which too
there was a Cavity filled with Lymph. Such are
fome of the material caufes of the fymptoms of
fenfe, intellectual powers, and voluntary motion.

As to the diftinction of apoplexies from thefe
different caufes; thofe from Sanguineous extravafations, or fudden fwellings of the Membranes give
very little notice, the Brain being fuddenly compreffed
by the fwelling, the fymptoms inftantly follow.
By extravafation the Brain is at at once overwhelm-
ed, and all voluntary motion almoft, if not altogether fuppreffed; but thofe from Serous exfuda-
tions, being formed by degrees, moftly fignify
themfelves by head-achs, vertigoes, drowfinefs,
numbnefs, and even refolution of fome of the Mufcles and fatuity *. And they alfo follow the errors
of inceffant and intemperate drinking, obftructions
to the difcharges of perfpiration and urine, or the
drying of an old ulcer whofe Ichor has diffufed itfelf in the Cortex, Membranes or Ventricles.

Sometimes apoplexies have been known to arife
from caufes not evident to fenfe by diffection. A
remarkable example of which is related by Willis †:
He found in an elderly gentiewoman, who was fud-

* Sir Edmond King, Tranf. Phil. vol. 3. 157.
† De anima brutorum, Oxon. 1672, p. 389.

denly

denly taken off with this diforder, neither fwelling
of the Membranes, Cortex, extravafated Blood,
Lymph, or ill conformation of Brain or Membranes,
nor any morbid difpofition or preternatural appearance in either of the other Venters. So that he af-
figns as the immediate caufe fome heterogeneous
materials depofited out of the Blood in the Brain,
which acted by extinguifhing the fpirits: and (to
me) not without reafon too; for if a drop from the
poifon-fangs of the Rattle-Snake * killed in a mi-
nute with fymptoms not very diffimilar, or the bite
of the creature called by Galen Phalangium, or Tur-
tur Marinus, or Scorpio Terrenus, can propagate
its deadly effects in an inftant, I fee no reafon but
fuch an humour might be fometimes generated in the
Blood and depofited in the Brain, and tho' fmall in
quantity yet great in Power (as Galen fays †) have a
fimilar effect. Whether that effect fhould arife
from a want of that which is conveyed through the
nervous Fibres and Membranes of the fyftem, as in
the cafe of extinction; or from a fudden and univerfal fpafm of the fame parts into which they might
be thrown by the action of that humour on the ethereal medium of the medullary Tracts and Fibres of
the Nerves; at leaft I fee no contradiction in it.

Now, if thefe and fuch obfervations are duly confidered, we may readily infer how ufeful and effec-
tual inftantaneous and copious bleeding may be in
fudden apoplexies ‡ from internal caufes; and efpe-

---

* Sir Hans Sloane, Idem, vol. 9. 55.   † Galen de locis
affectis, lib. 3. C. 5. et lib. 6. 5. ‡ Hildanus, Cent. 6. Obf. 12.
Franckfort. 1682, fol.   .

cially

cially if (from the florid and turgid complexion of the person, his short Neck, whose Muscles are likewise environed with fat, his full feeding, drinking repeatedly, violent passion of joy or surprize by whose actions on the nervous parts too much Blood may be thrown on the Brain, want of exercise to carry off the load, or break down the Grumes into which the Blood of the infarcted vessels may be apt to run) there is reason to think this Venter is loaded with blood : For all fullness of this Organ is to be held much more dangerous than a fullness of any other, as the very compression of the medullary tracts, which easily yield from the softness of texture, suspends all communication between the Organ and the rest of the system, which is immediately necessary to the life of the person; exclusive of the possible and desperate consequence of extravasation. And even if the cause should be extravasated Lymph, the emptying the vessels by copious bleeding may relieve the Brain for the present, and possibly contribute somewhat to its resorption, provided the effusion of it be recent. Dr. Gibbons † of Oxford cured one held deplorable, by taking away sixty ounces at once, which by the most exact estimations may be five ninths of the Blood contained in the vessels when they are moderately full. And Cole himself cured a Vertigo remaining from an attack of an apoplexy in a Lady of seventy-seven years old, by taking thirty ounces at once, and in a week after as much. Beside this immediate and plentiful depletion, it is also requisite to add a very stimulating

† Cole on Apoplexies, Oxon. 1689. p. 173.

Clyster

Clyfter of fudden operation, fuch as warm water
with a fourth or a third part of Tincture of Jalap or
of the antimonial Wine; and at the fame time two
fcruples or half a drachm of the compound powder of
Scammony out of fome fimple or fpirituous water,
and given by fpoonsful, in order to clear the whole
inteftinal Canal; for by thefe means the Blood of the
Mefenterick Arteries having an eafier flux through
the Membranes of the Inteftines and Mefentery, than
when they were compreffed by the Repletion, the Velocity in the defcending Aorta above thefe veffels will
be thereby accelerated by the removal of the refiftance
of the columns of Blood in thefe Arteries. Befides
the preffure on the Trunk of the defcending Aorta
by the Inteftines being removed, the Blood will
run down the Spine and Iliacs with the greater freedom, and in confequence of all this the derivation
from the Carotids and Vertebrals will be very confiderable : Thus you will obferve how clear and light
the Head will often become in fevers from the exhibition of Clyfters, of which phænomenon this
this feems no irrational account.

Befides the foregoing proceedings, it will alfo be
expedient to lay Blifters on the Neck, Shoulders
and Legs; a fevere though a juft proceeding; for the
falts of the flies getting into the Blood, by their mix-
ture with it will draw the attracting Globules afunder,
the Globules being more ftrongly attracted by the
Salts than by each other; and by their ftimulus on
the fenfible and irritable Fibres will raife the Vibrations of the Membranes, and in confequence acce-
lerate the Fluids they contain, which acceleration
will

will be propagated throughout all the nervous Membranes by confent. And fhould the apoplexy be of the ferous kind, the derivation of Lymph from the origins of the Nerves muft needs be of fignal ufe.

There is alfo another way of ftimulus, by Cautery, which may be tried if neceffity require; for if the Skin be touched near the Neck, or any other part therewith, as being a nervous and fenfible Membrane, it will foon tranfmit its feeling to the Brain, if there is any life at all remaining, and roufe it to a fucceffion of the obftructing Matter.

Laftly, if by thefe feverities we are fo lucky to get over the fit, then nature may be affifted with fpirituous cordials: Such are Pennyroyal or Cinnamon fimple waters, with a fourth or thereabouts of compound fpirits of Lavender, a twentieth of fpirits of Harts-horn or the volatile Aromatic fpirit, given at fmall intervals and repeatedly by fpoonsful.

Among the antecedent caufes we have affigned above, are full feeding, an inactive life, want of due difcharges, and fudden paffions of the mind: But the Air itfelf has been obferved productive of this diforder in the epidemical apoplexy in England about the year 1688, and that by its fenfible quality cold. The reafon of which feems to be, that the Skin is fo conftricted as not to fuffer the due proportion of vapour to exhale, and if fome other Gland does not officiate for it, a plenitude muft be the natural confequence, provided the quantity of food is given during the time of this coldnefs from day to day; befide, the Fibres of the whole fyftem of Mufcles are fo tightened up, that their blood is driven into

the

the interior parts and Membranes, infomuch that
they are inundated therewith; and if this conftitution of the Air continue for a time, the Heart and
internal Membranes may, from their oppreffion, be
rendered wholly unable to return it into the parts
above the Bones. As to the conftitution and make
of parts liable (cæteris paribus) to this diforder, that
of a fhort Neck has been obferved, yet I do not re-
member any reafon affigned why it fhould be productive of it. The reafon may be, that the appulfe
of the Blood is quicker on the Brain (cæteris paribus) than where the Neck is longer; for inftance, let
F exprefs the force of the Heart, L the length of the
Carotides and Vertebrals, D their diameter: Now
it is demonftrable, from the doctrine of Hydrau-
licks, that the velocity in Pipes is $\dfrac{v-F}{v-DL}$ therefore
when F and D are given the velocity will be as $\dfrac{1}{v-L}$.
Now if the Appulfe is quicker at every fyftole of the
Heart, the fwelling in confequence of the Membrane and Cortex will be more fudden, and efpecially if the Egrefs of the Blood is any way retarded
by the compreffion of the Fat upon the Veins defcending from the Head.

Hitherto we have confidered the antecedent and
immediate caufes of this diforder, let us now trace
the confequential effects: When the fit is difcuffed,
the veffels of the Membranes and Cortex are often
left fomewhat dilated and defective of their juft Elafticity; moreover by the fwelling antecedent, the relative pofitions of the medullary tracts are probably
changed

changed among themfelves; and it is by this dilatation and change of relative pofition, that the veffels are fo liable to returns of obftruction, and the
actions of the *thinking thing* which is within us are
often impeded, as depending on the due fituation of
the medullary tracts: And thofe impediments are
manifeft by the vifible decay of apprehenfion, memory, reafon, and lively voluntary motion, of which
laft there is often left in fome part a total defect. And
if the fit were of the ferous kind, the Membranes,
and the Brain itfelf, are left fo moift, that they are as
liable to returns and other imperfections, as if from
the expanfion of the veffels in the other kind; the
Vibrations being thereby lefs vivid.

In this cafe, the cure will partly depend on diet
and partly on medicines. The ufe of any medicine intended to reftore elafticity to dilated Fibres,
or dry the humid Membranes, is vain. But it is evident, that by whatever means the veffels of the
parts can be conftantly emptied or preferved from
intumefcence, that by perfeverance in the care thereof, the veffels of the Cortex may recover their
tightnefs, and the medullary tracts their relative pofitions among themfelves: But the veffels can be
kept from fwelling again only by detracting from
the diet or encreafing the difcharges; of which the
former is by much the more eligible, as carrying
with it an uniformity and certitude the others are
incapable of. If a man's diet in a natural day be
five pounds, or fixty ounces troy, and he detract a
fifth, and the fum of the Secretions be to the food
ftill in a given proportion, and the Secretions alfo
to

to each are invariable, then will every part lofe in proportion to its fize; and if thefe methods are continued, the loaded part will at length recover itfelf: And if the drink is leffened in a greater proportion than the folid food, the fwelling or dilatation will not only fubfide, but the Membranes or the Cortex, being drier by thefe means, will be the more difpofed to reimbibe any fluid which may there extravafate. But as there are fome who are ufed to intemperance, to whom this perfeverance would be worfe than death, then the encreafing the difcharges is the only way; which is done either by bleeding, as Cole did, or repeated purging with fome warm tincture, as Tinctura Sacra with a fourth of tincture of Senna, or any other of like power: For Diureticks, which have that power without adding to the quantity of Serum, can be fcarcely relied on, as they lofe their ftimulating powers moftly before they arrive at the Kidnies.

In all the foregoing cafes, we have feen that paralytick affections, having their caufes within the Skull, are attended with drowfinefs or other change in the powers of the underftanding; that is, the mind, having loft its power of propagating its influence to the exterior ends of the Nerves, fo alfo has it of receiving impreffions at the ends of the Nerves, with the vivacity it ought to do, or reafoning duly about what it has fcarcely and flowly received. Whence we may fafely fay that paralytick affections, with perfect underftanding, have their caufes rather exiftent in the Medulla Ob-

longata

longata and Spine, and poffibly in the Cerebellum.
Now thefe caufes are fuch as produce a Paralyfis of
the whole man, but differ in this, that the permanent fwellings in the Membranes or Cortex of thefe
parts, or extravafation of Blood or Lymph, is lefs
diffufive than in the firft; and the idea is juft the
fame, fubftituting only vertebral Sinufes * and arterial Rings within the Spine, for Carotids and vertebral Arteries and Plexufes, and venal Sinufes in
the Head ; and though treated juft in the fame way,
yet they are often difficult of cure, partly for the
impoffibility of abforbing extravafations of Blood,
and the difficulty of imbibing the Serum, or dif-
cuffing the materials congefted in the Membranes
where the Nerves of the parts arife.

It was by leffening his diet, and changing the
proportion of his drink to his folid food, that the
late Dr. Robinfon † cured himfelf of a paralytick
diforder in the year 1744. His weight, being
then 164 pounds, by leffening his food in the proportion of eighty-fix to fifty-eight, his drink a third,
and folid a fixth, and perfevering in it, he loft of
his weight in 17 months twenty pounds : Now the
proportion of lofs in the Head and Spine carried
with it the weight with which the Nerves and their
origins were loaded and oppreffed; which, by the
reafons above, very probably arofe from Congeftion
not extravafated, and which had not broke the
medullary texture of the Spinal Marrow or its ori-

* Willis Cerebi Anatome, fub finem, Oxon. 1664. 4to.
† Food and Dicharges, p. 35. 61.

gin,

gin, the Medulla Oblongata, between the Brain and it.

Hitherto I have not confidered either the quality of the Blood, or the Fibres of the Mufcles, among the caufes of paralytick diforders ; it is true, that when the Fibres are foaked in Serofities, being thereby relaxed and weakened, they lofe their elaf-ticity, but the effect of that lofs will be rather an impotent or weak tremulous motion, as in St. Vitus's Dance*, than what is properly called a Paralyfis : For take a limb truly paralytick in your Hand, weigh it, and the fenfe of the weight is fuch as of the whole quantity of the limb ; but weigh a limb rather weak than paralytick, and you will find a perception of a caufe counteracting the gravity, it falling towards you only with the excefs of gravity above that caufe.

As to the poverty of the Blood, by which it may be conceived unable to fupply the Brain with fpi-rituous fluid, if that Poverty be univerfal through the whole Mafs, as it muft, then will all parts of the Brain be equally deftitute of fpirituous fluid, and the whole fyftem of Nerves and Fibres of the Muf-cles in confequence ; and thus will the whole man fall down Apoplectick. If the Blood be equally fizy throughout, the fame may arife from a total obftruction of the Membranes and Cortex, pro-vided the Membranes and Cortex are in an uniform aptitude to be obftructed ; but if the Blood be un-equally fizy, then may fome of the Lentors ftop,

* Galen de tremore.

infarct

infarct and swell a part of the Membranes or Cortex, the consequence of which may be a Paralysis of some part as before observed: Herein I consider the quality of the Blood only so far as it causes obstructions or extravasation by erosion; and the Fibres only so far as their impotence may arise from want of due nutrition, which follows the obstructions of their Nerves.

In the second, sixth, and ninth Observations the purulent Matter, distilling from the Diploe, shewed an extravasation, and possibility of Apostems forming in the Bones: For that the Bones are vascular we may infer from this; and further from their being tinged, by dieting Creatures with madder root * in their food, the black jaundice †, and yet further from the injections of Ruscius, and the preparations of Dr. Hunter and Mr. Cleghorn, which being transparent you may see the lines of the Vessels through the Lamellæ of the Bones.

In the ninth Observation we have seen that the Causes of an Epilepsy are one or more Abscesses in the Dura Mater, and that not by any Spasm in the Membranes, which we have shewn impossible; but rather by its Ichor dripping on the Pia Mater, or its vapour expiring toward, and by its irritation disturbing, the Brain, through that Membrane.

Of other Causes of Epilepsies discovered by dissection are Lymph extravasate about the Cerebellum (*posticam Capitis partem*), induration of the Cerebrum, and connection with the Dura Mater, and

---

* Transf. Phil. vol. 9. p. 102.
† Mead Præcept. Med. cap. 9.

extra-

extravafation of Lymph, within the Pia Mater, Cerebrum, and in the Ventricles; which growing acrid by ftagnation or effervefcing as Pifo * conceives, produces thofe undulations in the Nerves, the Caufes of the Fits: So alfo are Caufes acting on the Nervous Membranes at a Diftance from the origins of the Nerves, whofe effect is propagated in power to the Brain and reflected to the Mufcles, or internal Nervous Parts; fuch are worms in the Inteftines, Urine pent up in the Ureter †, or kept in the fyftem by want of power in the Kidnies to fecern ‡, and by its irritation acting like the extravafated Lymph obferved by Pifo.

And it univerfally appears, that however the motion of the Heart may fometime continue independant of the Brain, yet the fyftem willfoon grow cold, inert, and fpiritlefs, for want of whatever it is that it derives from this fun of the Microcofm.

* Pifo de Morb. a Serofa Colluvie, p. 140, Edit Paris. 1663.

† Tran. Phil. v. 7. 486.

‡ Ridley Obferv. 30. Lond. 1703.

‖ Hoadly on Refpiration, p. 99 Lond. 1740.

SECT.

SECT. II.

Of the NECK and CHEST.

OBSERVATION I.

Quincy from a Swelling of the Larynx.

THE old Man * tells us, that in a Quincy or fenfe of fuffocation, it is an ill fign when no intumefcence appears either in the mouth or exter- nally; and Galen † affirms, that when there is a ftrong elevation of the Spine and Cheft in the act of infpiration, and the heat of the Cheft is moderate, it fignifies a ftricture of the Inftruments of refpiration; and that it is fometimes caufed by a refolution of the Mufcles of refpiration, which laft kind I have feen myfelf lately in an Hemiplectick

* Progn. & Coacæ Prænot.
† De Loc. affect. l. 4. c. 3. 5.

Perfon;

Perfon; but the diffections of later times have found, befides the intumefcence of the Uvula, Tonfils, and Mufcles of the Neck from Blood or Lymph, either in their Veffels, or extravafated into their interftices, that a Quincy is caufed by fwelling of the Epiglottis, Membranes of the Rimula, and Larynx. Reafon has alfo traced its caufe exiftent near the origin of the Nerves of the Larynx, which by irritation of the Nerves has thrown its Mufcles into fpafms; or by irritation of the Trachea in the mode of natural perception* has produced a fimilar effect.

A man about thirty came to Steevens's in December 1755, with a very laborious breathing, ufing a ftrong extenfion of the Spine and elevation of the Cheft at every infpiration; but his expirations were eafy, being paffive, and as it were a remiffion of infpiration only. His voice was fharp and low,

* Gliffon de Natura Subftantiæ, c. 15. & de Ventriculo, &c. c. 7.

but audible and clear, no swelling appeared either in the mouth or externally; his pulse not irregular, excepting that you might feel an intermission sometimes. He was free from pain, internal heat, or fever, and walked about the hospital the first, second, third, and fourth of December, and played at cards in the evening: On the fifth in the morning he was suddenly suffocated.

In removing the Muscles of the Larynx they did not appear in the least intumified; nor was there any Lymph extravasated in the interstices of the fibres, nor any swelling within the Mouth evident to sense; but on taking out the Larynx the Epiglottis appeared swelled, soft, and œdematous, so also were the Artenoid Cartilages, and Membranes forming the Rimula. On spliting open the Cricoid Cartilage, the Membrane lining the Larynx appeared very much swelled and œdematous, but not red; the Membrane of the Air Pipe was quite red, as if filled with a very fine injection, and so down

through

through the Lungs as far as we could trace; the right Lobes of the Lungs adhered to the Pleura, Mediaſtinum, and Diaphragm univerſally.

Now as there was no internal heat or fever we could not ſay the Lungs and their Membranes were inflamed, though they adhered to the Membranes of the Cheſt as parts in a ſtate of inflammation are wont to do; but that the Membrane of the Air Pipe and its branches were inflamed, was evident to ſenſe; ſo the Trachea may be inflamed, independent of the reſt of the Lungs; but the ſoft ſwellings of the Larynx were the immediate cauſe of his death, the afflux of Lymph cloſing the Rimula, inſpiration was cohibited thereby.

Thus repeated Defluxions on theſe parts may, by the Fibres of the Membranes loſing their elaſticity, induce a permanent Oedema, and effect ſuffocation. The weakened Fibres yield to every ſucceeding defluxion, being unable to expreſs the additional congeſtion; and as the interior membrane of the Inteſtine in an habitual dyſentery, ſo will the Membrane of the Trachea ſometimes from repeated inflammation and fluxion, looſen from the pipe in the act of coughing, and cauſe inſtantaneous death. It was the principal part affected in the fever epidemical in Cornwall in the year 1749, which proved fatal almoſt to every one, and eſpecially thoſe of younger ages. Sometimes too the Mucus of the Trachea, when the fluxion is great, not very acrid and

and repeated, will be fo infpiffated on the Membrane, that it has been coughed up refembling the Membrane, or a Veffel of the Lungs, as in the Cafes related by Tulpius *, Loffius †, Samber ‡, and Nichols, and thereby the perfon happily relieved.

Hence we may infer the ufe and even neceffity of Blifters on the fides of the Neck, and the whole Larynx, after general evacuations by Bleeding, Purging, Sweating, and Blifters on the Back, in Quincies where the Larynx and its Membrane are the parts affected, fuch as were directed by the late Mead ‖.

The antecedent caufes of fwellings in the Larynx are either the confinement of the vapour exhaling from the Neck, as in fudden accefs of cold air; or going againft a wind uniformly blowing on the Neck, without fufficient covering; or too great a proportion of folid to fluid in Diet, by which the Blood, not fufficiently diluted, runs into Lentors, and ftops in parts apt to be obftructed; the veffels being charged with unaffimilated fluid, yielding materials for fluxion, principally caufed by want of juft proportion of the Sum of the difcharges to food in a given time.

Afthma from an Induration of the Lungs.

Hippocrates § fays, that if the Lungs grow dry and do not expectorate, they

---

* Lib. 2. c. 13.   † Lib. 2. Obf. 13.   ‡ Tran. Phil. vol. 7. 564.   ‖ Præcept. Med. §. 94. 1754.   § De Morb.

harden,

harden, and terminate in death: And
Galen * difcerns a Shortnefs of Breath
from a fuppuration or fluxions in the
Treachea by the wheefing, and from
an induration by its increafe without
wheefing. How far an induration of
the Lungs may extend, together with
its fymptoms and effects, the following
obfervation will demonftrate.

OBSERVATION II.

In winter **1753,** a man about fifty,
tall and corpulent, coachman to one
of the phyficians of the hofpital, came
to St. George's in London. He had a
Shortnefs of Breath for many years, unaltered in all pofitions of the Trunk,
and without Hydropical Swellings in
his Legs. After taking repeatedly the
moft approved medicines, as well before he came to the houfe as after his
acceffion, he tired of them all, and
died toward the end of November.

* De Loc. affect. l. 4. c. 7.

In

In the right fide of the Cheft there
was fome extravafed water of a dilute
red Colour; and a hole in that lobe
as large as an orange; in the left fide
there was no water, but the Lungs
were hardened into a rude inorganical
mafs, without Membranes or Veffels,
or Fluids: In the pulmonary Artery
there was a polypous concretion of the
thicknefs of a goofe quill, in colour
white and red intermixed, and branched; and the Pericardium filled and
diftended with water.

Now as one half of the Lungs were fo obftructed
that no Fluids could move there, and a fixth (fup-
pofe) of the other half broke up and confumed,
there remained but two fixths or one third of the
Lungs for the Blood to move through; fo that a
man may live fome time with lefs than one half of
the Lungs continuing unobftructed.

A fhortnefs of breath perfifting for years, and
nearly the fame in all pofitions of the Trunk with
refpect to the Horizon, and without Hydropical
Swellings of the Legs, may fometimes indicate an
induration of the Lungs; and agreeable to Galen's defcription it was unattended with wheefing
(*ftertore*).

- Indurations

Indurations of the Lungs may arise either by fluxions infpiffating in the Bronchiæ, which by degrees obftruct the finer branches of the pipe, and the reft in fucceffion, or by Lentors ftopping in the Bronchial Arteries that fwell the Tunics of the Pulmonary Veffels, firft near their extremities, an in fucceffion near the heart; or laftly by Lentors ftopping near the extremities of the Pulmonary Artery, though I believe but feldom, by reafon of the rapid motion of the Blood through the Lungs*. But in all thefe incipient obftructions an aptitude in the Fibres of the Tunics is required either fupervenient or native; fuch are a want of elafticity, or too rigid a ftate, either of which are attended with vibrations too feeble for expreffing the materials of incipient infarctions.

That obftructions of the Lungs fometimes commence in the Air Pipe we may argue from their being coughed up in the form of the Trachea; and that they begin in the Pulmonary Artery, fometimes we have feen in this obfervation.

Afthmas are alfo caufed by induration and thickning of the Pleura; Pus between the Intercoftals and Pleura, in the Mediaftinum, and Cavities; ftones in the Lungs; preffure of the Diaphragm by fwelled Liver and Spleen, or enlarged by unequal nutrition, induration of, and enlargement of the Glands in or upon the Trachea; and thefe caufes are permanent and without intermiffion, and are difcovered by diffection; and reafon has alfo difcovered their caufes near the origin and termination of the

* Hales's Hæm. Exp. 10 63.

Nerves,

Nerves, of the Lungs and Mufcles of refpiration, exciting fudden undulations in their ethereal medium; in the Blood itfelf, which either by Lentors infarcting, or turgefcence from rarefaction, or quantity by reafon of full feeding and fmall difcharges, and in the thicknefs of the veffels by over nutrition of their Fibres, correfponding to fuch affections in the Liver and Spleen.

Since Afthmas then may terminate in fuch changes of the Lungs as in the obfervation, may we not infer the great ufe of fuch means when this diforder is forming as are known to keep the Blood's motion brifk through the Lungs, and the whole fyftem; fuch are conftant riding, if the bufinefs of the perfon will admit; for thus fluxions are inhibited to fubfide on, and line the Membrane of the Air Pipes, and the fuperfluity of the humidity in the whole fyftem driven off through the Skin and Kidnies; and the congeftions fubfiding in the Bronchiæ by a more ftrong and diffufive exhaling of the vapour in the Lungs, are thinned, diffolved, and, by the ftrength and quicknefs of refpiration carried off; and by the fame means fizy Blood or Lentors are cohibited from uniting with the Fibres, from the languor of their motion : But fhould it happen either from the avocation of the man, or fome indifpofition of another part, that the cure by riding cannot be complied with, Emetics now and then, with a moderate operation, will exceedingly contribute ; for in the operation of Emetics the Mufcles of the Belly are drawn by confent with the Stomach into ftrong fpafms; and by the repeated fuccuffions the con-

tents

tents of the Belly are forced on the Diaphragm, which motion communicated to the Lungs, they are enabled therewith to exprefs their incipient congeftions : But if the agitation of vomiting be from peculiar difpofition infupportable, as it fometimes is, then Emetics may be fo contrived as to keep up a gentle working in the Stomach, lefs than fufficient for a total ejection of its contents, which will have nearly an equal effect.   And if both thefe ways are attended with averfion, the motion of the Cheft may be raifed by fwinging irons with leads appended, which by the alternate elevation and depreffion of the Cheft will communicate a motion to the Lungs additional to their own ; fo alfo will playing on the German flute or other wind inftrument, which increafes the number and ftrength of expirations in a given time.   But all thefe mechanical effections ought to commence with the fymptoms, before tubercles of any fize, ulcers, or fuppurating tumours have time to form, and efpecially vomiting ; for if from the time of continuance and the other fymptoms there is caufe to fufpect fuch a change of conformation as in the obfervation, then reafon tells us, that vomits are fo far from giving relief, that they may effect an impreffion on the Lungs much to the detriment of the perfon; and the fame may be argued when there is reafon to fufpect water or any purulent colluvies between the Ribs and Pleura, at large in the Cavity, or in the Mediaftinum, or other immutable caufes we mentioned above.

Water

Water in the Pericardium was concomitant with this Obstruction in the Lungs. Probably for this reason, that the motion in the Pulmonary Arteries being more languid than it ought for a long succession of time, and in consequence of the right Ventricle and Auricle, the Blood coming from the coronary Vein, being somewhat retarded, did by persistence and easy delay dilate the Tunics of the Veins on the Membrane, and let the Lymph infiltrate.

OBSERVATION III.

Dropsy in one Cavity of the Chest.

Wilson was thirty years old in the year 1755, and from a cold in the winter complained of flying pains through the Muscles and Membranes of the Chest, which ended at length in a fixed pain of the left Side. From this time he languished and wasted with a slow fever. In February 1757 he began to breathe with difficulty, found an unusual weight when he lay on the right Side; and when he lay on the left he was also disturbed by a short troublesome cough; but was far most easy when he turned himself prone.

prone.   The left fide of the Cheft was
fomewhat enlarged : The urine fmall
in Quantity, with a white Recrement.
There was no intermiffion of the Pulfe,
nor preternatural beating of the Heart,
but what you might expect in a flow
febrile commotion.   We took him by
the fhoulders and fhook him, and heard
the undulation of fomething fluid in
the Cheft.   After due evacuations,
which fomewhat relieved him, an aperture was made between the third and
fourth Rib, computing from below;
and about three pints of a ferous colluvies drawn off : But this was fucceeded
by fo violent a fit of coughing and
fenfe of fuffocation, that Mr. Blundell
the furgeon was obliged to ftop the
aperture to prevent a total Suffocation.
The flow fever continuing, we gave him
half a drachm of the bark three times
a day till the fourth of March, when the
fever intermitted.   On the feventh the
wound, which had hitherto a cadaverous
appearance, began to digeft.   On the
ninth

ninth the fever returned, and fo continued till the 26th, when he died.

A poffible confequence then of a neglected pleu-
rify is a dropfy of the Cheft. With refpect to the
mode by which it was effected we may gather from
the antecedent caufe, (for we were not permitted to
infpect the contents of the Cheft) of catching cold,
the immediate one of painful obftructions in the
Membranes of the Cheft, the flow fever, and the
white fubfidence in the urine, that an ulcer exiftent
in the Pleura did by dripping its Ichor, fill the
Cavity. Thus alfo from the fituation of the ulcer on
the interior furface of the Ribs, the exterior furface
of the Pleura, or between the Membranes of the
Mediaftinum, may a dropfy between the Intercoftals
and Pleura, or in the Mediaftinum, be effected: But
fhould it be doubted that an Ulcer can yield fuch a
multitude of Ichor, let it drop into the Cavity once
in half an hour; then in twelve hours will it drop
twenty-four times; in three natural days, two
drachms; in a week, half an ounce; in a month,
two ounces; and in twenty-four months, forty-eight
ounces, which is equal to three pints.

It appears moreover, the fymptoms of the exiftence of water in one fide of the Cheft are an uneafinefs
and fenfe of weight in lying on the oppofite, and
the undulation audible by fhaking the Cheft. But
this laft fympt om, though decifive of extravafation,
is by no means of neceffity connected with it; for
when

when the cavity is full and the fluid thick, there will be no fluctuation, as the old man has obferved *.

We may alfo note, that the bark will take off an indifpofition of the Blood, which procceds from diftempered Membranes; but as the caufe fubfifts, the taint and fever confequently will return; and that it will bring about a digeftion in an ill-conditioned wound, whofe fibres have a cadaverous appearance.

OBSERVATION IV.

Dropfy in both Cavities.

In March 1753, came to Steevens's, a woman about 20, corpulent and florid: fhe had a very difficult and laborious breathing, a great oppreffion and dejectednefs; to thefe fymptoms fucceeded anafarcous fwellings in her legs: her pulfe was depreffed and intermitted, purgers of water relieved her at times, yet the Serum tranfuded from the Membranes of the Cavity, notwithftanding thefe derivations. At length fhe became univerfally anafarcous, and

* Coacæ prænot.

the

the fhortnefs of breath increafing, fhe
could not lie down: her Pulfe oftener
intermitted, and funk fo low that it
was fcarce perceptible. Laftly, fhe
coughed up Blood, and died the 25th
of the fame month.

The Cheft was enlarged on both
fides. In removing the Sternum the
water jetted up a foot in height, as foon
as ever the Intercoftals and Pleura were
pierced. The removal of the Sternum
exhibited both fides of the Cheft filled
with water. The lower Belly was alfo
full; and the Cellular Membrane of
the Mufcles every where. Nor could
we difcern any change of ill conformation any where, either in the Cheft or
lower Belly. The Auricles and Ventricles, or great veffels of the Lungs, we
were not fuffered to infpect.

A Shortnefs of breath then, nearly the fame in the
beginning for any given time, and in all fituations of
the trunk, excepting fupine, and that towards the
end, attended with an intermiffion of the Pulfe, an
enlargement of the whole Cheft, and fucceeded with
ferous fwellings of the Legs, are fymptoms of the
exiftence of water extravafate in both Cavities of the
　　　　　Cheft:

Cheſt: the ſhortneſs of breath indicates a ſtricture
on the Bronchiæ, the depreſſed and intermittent
Pulſe a preſſure on the veſſels of the Lungs, and the
hydropical ſwellings of the Legs obſtructions to the
free aſcent of the Blood from the Iliac Veins receiving
and returning the Blood from the inferior extremities, and the enlargement of the Cheſt the fulneſs of
the cavities.

It appears moreover that water will ſometimes
perſiſt to accumulate by ſucceſſive effuſion; that it
will at length ſo preſs the Lungs as to force the Blood
into the Bronchiæ and ſuffocate.

Until the exiſtence of Lymphaticks in the human
ſubject ſhall be more generally agreed on, and the
preſſure, eroſion, or rupture they may ſuſtain from
Tumors in the Membranes of the Lungs, or quality, quantity, or motion of the Lymph flowing
therein, the following hypotheſis will ſerve, till repeated diſſection ſhall either ſettle or reject it *.
Let any cauſe preſs the common Vein into which
the Veins of the Cheſt unload themſelves, then is it
evident the tunics of thoſe Veins will be rarer at their
origins in the Membranes than they were before,
and will be diſpoſed thereby to let their Lymph infiltrate; and the place of extravaſation may be any
of the ſpaces mentioned in the laſt obſervation. Probably the Pleura may ſometimes ſwell and thicken ſo
as to effect this preſſure when the Membrane is the
part affected in the pleuriſy, where the pain is near

* Vid. Morgagnia adverſ. anatom. in Diſſer. de ven. ſine
pari. p. 86. Leidæ. 1723.

5

the Vertebræ of the Back, and on the right Side ; or
even on the left, if fuch a Vein exift on this fide,
which has been fometimes obferved : and extravafation may arife from a fwelling of the Membrane of
the Lungs, where the Azygos croffes and defcends
to the Cava.   The like mode of effeคtion may likewife proceed from intumefcenfe of lentors or cold
congeftions in the fame Membranes ; or the fwelling of the pleura might in places, at a diftance from
that where the Azygos paffes, prefs the Intercoftal
Veins to a fimilar effeคt ; or partial coalefcence may
happen in the Azygos, by a fwelling of its Tunics,
like as it does in the Nafal duคt in the difeafe of
Lachrymal Fiftula.   Sharp on Operations, C. 30.

Again, fhould the Blood be obftruคted frequently
in paffing from the pulmonary Veins into the left
Auricle, as where the Auricle or its Ventricle are
partly infarคted with a polypous concretion* ; or when
the valves of the Auricle or the Ventricle are offified,
petrified, or otherwife indurated †, the Lungs and
their Membrane will as often fwell, and by fwelling
diffufe the Lymph through their Membranes, even
to exfudance, and fo may the Cavities fill from thefe
Caufes ; and yet more, if the fyftem is overcharged
with Lymph by obftruคtions in the Skin, Kidnies ‡,
or Membrane of the Trachea : And truly reafon
would incline one to think a dropfy of the Cheft
ought rather to be effeคted from thefe caufes, than
a dropfy of any other part ; for when the fyftem is

* Mead Præcep. med. 129. 1751, Lond.   † Cooper
Tranf. Phil. v. 5. 220.   ‡ Idem in eodem loco.

tumid

tumid with Lymph, the Lungs ought to find a more
fenfible impreffion of it than any part, as the whole
of what exifts in the Veffels muft repeatedly crowd
through the Vifcus, which is not a contingence elfewhere; and this will fooner happen in Gibbofities or
Incurvations of the Spine and Sternum, by reafon of
the flower motion of the Blood down the aorta, affu-
ming the flexure of the Spine. Now fhould the
Lymph, fo confined in the fyftem, and flowing
through the Lungs, pafs off by the Trachea, the
fit ends with a copious catarrh and expectoration;
but if it extravafate into the Interftices of the Veffels,
the Afthma proceeding therefrom becomes habitual;
and if the blood in the repeated Syftole of the Vifcus be, as from a wet fpunge, expreffed from the
Membrane, the infiltration induces a dropfy of the
Cheft; and a dropfy of the Cheft thus formed, may
come fuddenly on, and more fo if the Membrane of
the Lungs is weaker conftituted than the other
Membranes of the fyftem.

That an univerfal dropfy fhould follow from a
dropfy of the Cheft, and be dependant thereon, is
not very difficult to fhew; for fince at every infpiration fpace is allowed for an additional exfudance,
in time the quantity of water will be fo increafed as
to raife the Ribs, and the preffure will be very great,
not only on the Lungs, but trunks of the Cavæ and
common venous receptacle of the Blood of the
Back, and Membranes of the Cheft : A preffure at
firft, though lefs than any given one, on the defcending Cava, will, by uninterrupted fucceffion, fwell
the Veins of the Neck and Face, and extravafate the

Lymph

Lymph in these parts, and in the superior extremities and Muscles of the Back; nay, in the internal Membranes of the Head and Spine themselves: And pressure on the common Vein of Azygos will have the same effect in the Muscles of the Back, Membranes, and parts where its branches arise: On the Cava ascending, will fill the Liver, and in consequence the Spleen, Mesentery, Intestines, and cavity of the Belly; and by retarding the Blood coming from the Iliac Veins, the inferior extremities, as we see in Gravidation; the truth of all which you will readily deduce from the anatomy of Veins.

Dropsies of the Chest are relieved from time to time by draining the water through the Intestines, whatever cause they may depend on; but when the relief from purging becomes insensible, or next to none, the Paracentesis is requisite to prevent suffocation. This total cure will turn on the Membranes of the Chest and Lungs, being free from any immutable distemper; as also from any incurable obstruction of the Skin, Kidnies, or Membrane of the Bronchiæ, by whose organical power and effection the system is dried; and because it is rarely the condition of the parts in this disorder, they are justly held by Physicians among the most unhappy of those to which we are liable. It is probable then, that when they admit of cure, they have arose from mere fulness of Serum, from Perspiration, Urine, or Vapour of the Bronchiæ being accidentally confined, whose Organs re-assuming their function, and draining the System of its superfluity of water, that which infiltrated through the Membranes of the Chest or

Lungs

Lungs has been re-abforbed ; for that it is poffible the Membranes of this Venter may imbibe water there extravafated, we may infer from the experiments of Mufgrave ; for having injected three pints and a quarter of warm water into the Cheft of a dog at different times, in the fpace of a month, found it all imbibed by the recovery of the creature from the fymptoms of diftrefs he fhewed at the time of injection *.

Mary Pane, about eighteen, in November 1762, at Mercer's, had from repeated colds a dropfy of the Cheft. When fhe came to the hofpital fhe was totally tumid, her Eyes watry, the Cheft elevated, a great oppreffion and fhortnefs of Breath, the Pulfe almoft imperceptible, and anafarcous fwellings of her Legs ; of all which affociation of fymptoms fhe was cured by repeated purging :. At leaft reafon, led by thefe fymptoms, their antecedent caufes and mode of cure, did conclude thefe fymptoms arofe from that caufe.

When the puncture is made to let out the water after what is in the cavity is drained, yet fhould the orifice ftill remain, left the clofing of it might, by the Cheft again filling, neceffitate a new aperture, as it did in the inftance related by Willis †.

---

* Tranf. Phil. vol. 3. 78.   † Pharm. Rat. 230. Oxon. 1675.

OBSERVATION V.

Hæmoptoe.

In October 1756, a Man about 30 years old, tall and lean, who had been ufed to all forts of exceffes in the antecedent caufes of difeafes, came to Steevens's with an Hæmoptoe: He coughed up Blood in large clots repeatedly in the day, without pain, and continued fo to do for three weeks, and died the 22d of the fame month. He had likewife a conftant difpofition to ftool, but with ineffectual efforts.

In the Lungs of both fides of his Cheft were large Grumes chiefly toward the back, an univerfal Echymofis vifible throughout the Membrane, and above a pound extravafate in the cavities ; the fmall Inteftines too were exceedingly enlarged and inflated, and the diameter of the Colon double of its due fize, which enlargements were

D 4   manifeft

manifest before the opening the body
as a Tympanites.

It is observable too that no part of
the Blood extravasated here had the
appearance of corruption.

An Hæmoptoe therefore may not only signify
that the Vessels of the Bronchiæ let go their Blood,
but that the same disposition may prevail throughout the whole Lungs, and even the Membrane
itself.

One cause of the extending and retarding the motions of the Intestines is, their being inflated with
vapour. * The Blood, according to authors, extravasates into the Bronchiæ by rupture, as in a violent fit of coughing, or from external incidents ; by
transudation ; or lastly, by aperture or enlargement
of the orifices opening into the Bronchiæ, and this
either by their natural terminations or adventitious
by erosion : But from the appearance of the Lungs
in this subject, wherein was a total confusion of
Fibres and Cruor, the Hæmoptoe was rather consequential of a dissolution of the Fibres, which let the
Blood extravasate as well into the Interstices of the
vessels as into the Chest and Bronchiæ. And its being unattended with pain signified its coming from
the substance of the Lungs by reason of the obtuse
sense of the Viscus, its Nerves not reaching the parts
near the surface or Membrane, as Galen observes †,

* Fernelius lib. 6. C. 10.   † Galen de loc. affect. lib. 4.
Cap. 4.

or

or probably fervient rather to the organical motion of the Vifcus, and vital union of the Lymph with the Fibres than fenfibility of the part.

Bleedings from the Lungs caufed by rupture, provided the ruptured **veffels** are not very large, are cured by repeated bleeding, to leffen the quantity in the whole fyftem, by which the ruptured veffels will be lefs extended ; and by leffening the diet in a given time, and changing its quality to a cooling one ; for by leffening the diet the Lungs will be kept from intumefcence, and by changing the quality of a cooling one, the rarity and turgefcence of the Blood will be lefs than in an oppofite diet ; and thus will the veffels collapfe by their emptinefs, and regain continuity by appofition.

Bleedings caufed **by erofion,** as when the fharp Ichor of an ulcer deftroys their tunics, are partly treated by fuffumigations, whereby the **digeftive** vapour of the rofins, gums, and balfams, coming into contact with the Ichor, abate its fharpnefs †, provided they are not too detergent ; and by medicines continued for a long time, which are held to give fuch a difpofition to the Blood and Lymph that the ulcer may loofe its fupply of ill quality, and receive digeftion from what fuceeeds, fuch are fperma ceti in any form, Locatellus's Balfam, and the like ; and dieting partly or altogether on new churned buttermilk, milk juft broke with churning, and affes milk, An Hæmoptoe from this caufe is diftinguifhed from

† Bennett Theat. Tabid. **excer. 30.** Mead. Frecept. Med. C. 1. Sect. 10.

the

the preceding by the errors antecedent of intemperance and colds, by the nature of the expectorated Blood which is mixed with purulent phlegm, and from the ftench of the vapour returning from the lungs.

An Hæmoptoe by mere tranfudation or aperture of the orifices terminating in the Bronchiæ, if caufed by rarity or turgefcence of the Blood and violent progreffion from drinking, exercife, or irritating matter hurrying the fyftem of irritable Membranes, is ftopped for the prefent by bleeding, reft, dilution of the irritating matter, and thofe medicines which infpiffate the Blood, conftringe the Fibres, and fufpend their Vibrations; fuch are fimple waters, foured with fpirit of vitriol, fanguis draconis, alum, the peruvian bark, and opiates.

But if the bleedings are the fimple effect of weak Fibres, as in thofe who are conftituted with weak Lungs, then are they treated more eligibly in the dietetic way. Fibres which are weak from native conftruction, medicines may aftringe, ftrengthen they cannot: befide the perpetual repetition of ineffectual medicines, takes away the appetite, hurts digeftion, and induces ill habits and diforders different from thofe they are intended to amend; therefore ought we rather to depend on temperance in quantity of food, abftinence from liquors overheating the Blood, too violent exercife, fudden paffions of the mind, and have careful regard to the times of fleep, fince Fibres grow out of the Blood chiefly in found fleep: As bleedings of this kind are more incident to youth, they preferve themfelves from dangerous Hæmorrhages

rhages till they advance into years, when the hardnefs of the Fibres cohibits thefe effluxes; as the Hæmorrhages are not only dangerous by their quantity, but quiefcence; for if the extravafated blood
reft below, it endangers apoftems, ulcers, flow fevers, and confumptions *.

It was in this ftate of weak Fibres (I conceive) that
vomits, fo luckily directed by the late Dr. Robinfon,
were attended with fuccefs; for vomits, though they
ftop the Motion of the heart, almoft totally in the act
of vomiting, yet after operation the motion rifes
higher than before, not only in the Lungs but even in
the whole fyftem; and by the total fuppreffion of the
motion in the act of vomiting it is, that the infiltration or effufion is checked for the prefent, and by
the increment of motion after operation it comes,
that the Blood moving ftronger through the great
veffels of the lungs, its courfe and tendency is derived from the veffels of or near the aperture, which
is eafily deducible from the doctrine of Hydraulicks,
and even by antopfy in the pellucid Membranes of
creatures; and I have myfelf often directed vomits
in Bleedings caufed by the erofion of Ichor, and obferved them fometimes of fervice, but never any
Hæmorrhage encreafed thereby. Yet in fudden and
great effufion from rupture or erofion of the Tunics
of great veffels, or where there is reafon to fufpect
a total echymofis or extravafation from the Membrane of the Lungs, one would incline to defer it
till all other means were tried, and even altogether.

* Hip. Aph. Sect 7. Aph. 15.   † Galen de præcogn. ex
pulfibus.

Ne videaris occidisse quem servare non potes *. But
if any one should say, how shall we conjecture this
to be the condition of the Lungs? you will easily
estimate by the persistance of the Hæmoptoe, and
grumous quality and quantity of the expectorated
Blood, compared with a constitution ruined by
colds, eternal drunkenness, and venery: For it is
evident that repeated colds filling the system with
acrid Lymph will shake the Lungs by the coughs
they occasion, and perpetual drinking will rarify the
Blood, and as often expand their Fibres whose nu-
tritious powers are weakened by excesses in venery,
and waking, all which were the errors of the miser-
able fellow whose Lungs we described.

And now we are speaking of the mode of action,
and one use of vomiting, it may not be totally foreign to the present purpose, to consider succinctly
their use in general. Vomits then can be of little
service (at least reason would incline us to think so)
in primary affections of the Head, such as produce
the symptoms of drowsiness, paralytick affections,
and epilepsies; but if any of those disorders should
arise from the Stomach by consent, as where the
Stomach is fretted with sharp bile, or other humor, phlegm, or crude undigested food, their use
here is evident; so likewise in recent infarctions of
the Lungs, either from sizy Blood or fluxions thickened in the Trachea, they far exceed the common
pectorals in their effects: so also in recent obstructions of the Blood or Bile Vessels in the Liver,
Spleen, or Mesentery; and universally they raise

* Celfus in Præfat.

the

the Blood's motion in the whole fyftem, even in the
Mufcles themfelves, and may be **of** fignal ufe in
languid motion from weak Fibres **and** fizy Blood in
all **parts,** and in removing fluxions (the gout for inftance) falling on the Membranes **of** the Cheft and
lower Belly ; due circumfpection had to the fullnefs
of the fyftem, and **to the** difpofitions of the parts,
that they **are free from** adherances, immoveable
obftructions, apoftems, ulcers, and preternatural
conformation, and the Cavities from extravafation.
Laftly with refpect to Bleeding in hæmorrhages of
the Lungs, the following obfervation may carry
with it a caution touching the **extent** of this mode
of proceeding.

OBSERVATION VI.

Dropfy anafarcous from Lofs of Blood.

In **March 1752,** a woman of forty-
eight was taken in at Steevens's for an
anafarcous Dropfy. About four years
before this time fhe coughed up Blood
from the Lungs **to** the quantity of
three or four pints in three days, and to
ftop it, nearly as much was taken **from**
the **arm** in the **fame time:** Thence-
forward her legs began to fwell, and
the water afcending fhe was inundated
there-

therewith, and died the later end of the fame month.

As a great lofs of Blood then may be attended with a dropfy, and efpecially in the female, and in the decline of life after moderate Bleeding in the arm or elfewhere, it were rather eligible to try what medicines which cool and infpiffate the Blood, and aftringe the Fibres, and check their vibrations can effect, than perfift in Bleeding, which, even if it ftop the prefent extravafation of Blood, may give origin to an equally fatal infiltration of Lymph.

OBSERVATION VII.

Empyema and *Apoftem of the Lungs.*

In September 1753, a boy about fourteen was brought to St. George's in London. About three weeks before he got a cold, and a violent cough, by changing his cloaths, and putting on a light unaired fuit. When he came to the hofpital his cough was rather lefs in degree; he breathed fo that you might hear the air in its tranfit pafs through fome tenacious matter, both in infpiration and expiration; he had a pain and forenefs in the right fide of his

his Cheft, and was somewhat incurvated that way; his countenance
sweaty, pale, and tumid; his pulse
quick, which quickness was increased
in the evenings; and in coughing he
brought up of thick tenacious matter
about half a pint in the day; and died
in three weeks from his coming to the
hospital.

Part of the right side of the Lungs
was confumed by an abscess, the matter of which was expended in the Cavity.

As the Lungs then may impostumate from a
cold and strong cough neglected at first, it should
seem as if the act of coughing did extravasate the
Blood in the Interstices of the Veffels, and the Blood
by corruption effected the impostume, or that the
act of nutrition or apposition of Lymph to the
Fibres being disturbed brought on a congestion,
which ended by putrefaction of the congested
matter; and that the impostume so formed did
communicate its corruption, as well to the parts
nearest, as to the Blood itself, which being tainted
therewith raised the flow fever, more observable in
the evening than at other times of the day; and the
symptoms of matter in the Lungs and Cavity are a
laboured respiration with a wheefing, a coughing
up of matter, and inclining of the Trunk toward
the

the part affected; a pale, tumid, fwelled countena ce, preceded by a cold and ftrong cough, and fucceeded by a flow fever, the cough being caufed by the vapour ftopped in the Skin, and exhaling in the Trachea, or by the acrid **Lymph** fecreted in the Glands of that irritable Membrane.

Since colds therefore by loading the Veffels with fcalding ferum and vapour, may caufe fuch agitations of the Lungs, we may deduce the utility in the beginning of colds and ftrong coughs, of leffening the quantity of Blood by Bleeding, which will alfo cool it, and of purging with cooling purges; fuch are infufions of rhubarb, fenna, and manna, in order to drain off the acrid ferum, and of fuch diaphoretics as have this power without heating, which the teftaceous powders given out of cold water fometimes have; abftinence from vinous and fpirituous liquors, and diet conferving the ill difpofition and heat of the Fluids; and we may further note, how cautious thofe who are conftituted with Lungs weak and liable to fluxion ought to be in changing their apparel.

Suppurations in the Cheft then are curable or not according to the circumftance. If the Cavity of the Cheft is full of Pus, which is known by the enlargement of the Cheft and flow fever, attending; and the Lungs, **Pleura**, **Mediaftinum**, **Intercoftals**, and Diaphragm are free from abfceffes, ulcers, and other morbid affections; and the Blood is not too faturate with pus by its long exiftence in the Cavity, the letting out the matter by incifion will prefently fucceed; but if the Lungs or their Membrane

brane have abfceded, which is known by the purulent expectoration and wheefing, and other fymptoms in the obfervation ; it is required they adhere
to the Pleura, and that it be fignified by the pricking pains in the act of coughing near the united
parts, and the external intumefcence and forenefs, fo
that the materials of the collection be drawn off by
the aperture ; for that abfceffes of the Lungs may
be thus totally cured, we may infer from the authority of **Cooper** * ; but if the apoftem is fituate in
the **Lungs**, and they do not adhere, or between
the Lungs and Diaphragm or Mediaftinum, and
the Lungs adhere round the Apoftem fo as to en-
cyft it, the cure will depend on fome effort of the
parts to caft it through the Larynx, or on the Veffels abforbing and transferring it through the Kidnies, or other fecreting organ, the poffibility of which
we have from the authority of Galen † ; and I have
feen it myfelf in a fuppuration of the Mufcles.

When by the aperture the tumor is apparently
drained, yet ftill, as in a dropfy of the Cheft, is it
proper to preferve an opening ; for if the Lungs
do not adhere, but the pus be at large in the Cavity, yet the Pleura, Diaphragm, Mediaftinum, or
Membrane of the Lungs, may by an ulcer there
exifting, drip fo as to occafion a new aperture.

Whether there are medicines which affift nature
in ejecting an apoftem of the Lungs, either through
the Larynx or Emunctories, has been fometimes
doubted ; but that medicines barely inoffenfive are
of ufe, is not only agreeable to experience, but rea-

* Tranf. Phil. vol. 5. 221.   † De Loc. affect. l. 6. 4.

fon,

son, which likewise holds in other difeafes, were it
no more than to calm the mind ; for when the mind
is at eafe, and not follicitous about the event, the
motions exerted will be more uniform and proportionable to the intent of nature, and fo more likely
to effect it.

But fometimes two fluxions, not fo acrid as the
vapour in the preceding, will either of themfelves
erode, or by exciting a conftant though not very
troublefome cough, fo difturb the nutrition of the
Fibres as to induce a congeftion, or by rupture, extravafation ; which ending by ulcer draws on an univerfal colliquefcence through the Vifcus, vifible by
the quantity of the expectorated matter ; and which
may be either of a black or variegated colour ; and
the materials of the ulcer being from time to time
re-abforbed by the Veffels, raifes the Blood into febrile effervefcences, correfponding in proportion to
inoculation ; and interior Membranes of the Heart
and other irritable Membranes into preternatural
vibrations, by which fanguification nutrition and
fecretion being diftributed, the Veffels are loaded with
heterogenous Fluid, which is repeatedly hurried off
through the Skin and Inteftines in form of colliquefcent fweats and loofenefs, fucceeded by an univerfal marafmus and diffolution of the fyftem.

OBSERVATION VIII.

Mary Tigh, about twenty-five years
old, from a cold contracted a cough,
which,

which, though not very violent, did by perfiftance in the fpace of four months draw with it a Marafmus, attended with a colliquefcence through the Lungs of varioufly coloured ftuff, fucceeded with repeated colliquefcent fweats and loofe-nefs, which brought her to her end at Mercer's, the 25th of October laft.

The right Lobes of the Lungs were variegated with black and white tubercles, the latter of which bore an exact fimilitude to condenfed fat; the left Lobes had feveral finuous ulcers larger than a middle fized peacod, and full of fuch vifcid, variegated colluvies which fhe conftantly ejected by coughing.

SECT. III.

Of the LIVER.

OBSERVATION I.

Suppuration in the Liver.

A Woman about fifty in 1756 came to Stevens's; five months before she had a Jaundice, and a fullnefs appeared in the region of the Stomach. The Jaundice difappearing, left the fwelling, which diffufed itfelf into both Hypochondria, and was attended with an internal heat and forenefs; fometimes too an acute pain was propagated from the right Hypochondrium to the fhoulder of the fame fide. She came in January, and toward the end of the month began to cough and fpit up a vifcid thick matter, of a very bitter tafte and intolerable ftench, about a

pint

pint in the day, and even skins of Hydatids. In the middle of February the spitting, which still continued, was attended with a loosenefs of the fame fort of matter, a wafting, and a fluttering intermittent pulfe, and all this perfifted till April, when she left the hofpital perfectly recovered, the tumor difappearing as she coughed up the matter.

The materials of a tumour in the Liver then, by the union of the Liver with the Diaphragm, and Diaphragm with the Lungs, affifted with motions inftituted by nature, may pafs the Lungs, and be emptied through the Larynx : For that it exifted in the Liver I infer from the jaundice appearing before the commencement of the fwelling, which shewed that fome caufe either preffed the Ducts near the Sinus of the Porta, or difturbed them in their motions, from the bitternefs of the ftuff coughed up, the pain propagated to the Shoulder *, and the appearance of hydatids, which are more obfervable in the Liver than Lungs, Tunics of the Colon, or Stomach. Now when the Liver is inflamed in its upper furface, or ulcerated, it will adhere to the Diaphragm, and inflame and ulcerate it ; and the like continuity of adherence may be between the Diaphragm and Lungs ; and thus by continued fuppuration, the matter, and even Skins of Hydatids,

---

* Hippocrat. lib. de Intern. Affect.

may

may find their exit by the Bronchiæ; so that we need not discredit Galen's * affirmation, that Pus or Blood in the Cavity of the Chest may be absorbed by the Membranes of this spongeous Viscus, and be ejected by the Larynx.

Besides our knowing how far the parts will sometimes exert themselves in their own defence, and free themselves from noxious materials, we may draw this useful inference, that in a similar case we may rather assist nature with soft pectorals to eject the filth, because we are assured of the possibility of motions instituted for this purpose being able to effect it, than proceed to immediate operation; for that which has once happened may return again.

OBSERVATION II.

Apostem of the Liver.

In September 1752 a man about twenty-five was brought to Stevens's; six weeks before, he arose from a continual fever which held him a fortnight, and terminated without crisis by sweats or other sensible secretion; from that time he had a pain and soreness in the right Hypochondrium, could not bear the least pressure on the part,

---

* De Meth. medendi, lib. 5.

and

and was somewhat incurvated that way: These symptoms were likewise attended with a loosenefs of white ftools, yet the urine was not preternatural in colour or otherwise; his countenance pale, languid, and yellow. In some days he was taken with a continual vomiting, and died the 25th of the same month.

On removing the Integuments and Mufcles of the Belly, we found the right fide of the Liver and Gall Bladder confumed by an abfcefs, the fluid of which was expanded in the Cavity.

A fever therefore, when the materials of it are not fecerned in a falutary crifis, as by the Skin, Kidnies, Salivary or other Glands, may poffibly terminate by a depofition of the matter on fome part, as the Liver, caufe it to inflame and fuppurate, and effect the apoftem termed Per Decubitum, and the fymptoms of it are a forenefs in the Hypochondrium, attended with a loofenefs, and an inclining of the Trunk toward the part affected. By this inclination of the Trunk the part affected refts on the parts underneath, a more eafy fituation than depending from the Diaphragm in an erect pofition of the Trunk, which keeps the tender ulcerated Fibres in a state of painful tension, the looseness being caused partly by the irritation of the matter lying on the Intestines, and partly by its passing through the Biliary Ducts into their Cavity; the white stools partly to a want of secretion of the Bile, and partly to the pus flowing into the Intestine and tinging its contents.

Impostumes in the Liver then are curable or not, according to the circumstances, like those of the Lungs, great Intestines, or other interior parts. If the apostem is in the center of the Liver, its cure will depend on some effort of the parts to take it up into the habit, and transfer it to the Kidnies, or other outlet, or on its breaking into the Intestines and passing off that way: But if it exist in the Tunic of the convex part, it may, by adherence with the Diaphragm, suppurate the Septum, and falling into the Cavity of the Chest, be drawn off by an aperture, or be taken up by the Lungs, and ejected through the Larynx, the possibility of which may be gathered from the preceding; but if the apostem exist in the fimbriæ of the Liver, it is required it unite with the Membrane of the Cavity, and from the suppuration of the Membrane signify itself by raising the Integuments, so that with proper applications it may thin the Integuments, and be drawn off by incision; but if it exist in the concave side of the Liver it may fall among the Intestines, and end as above.

Jaundice

Jaundice and other Effects of Stones in the Gall Bladder.

If the bile be difpofed to form ftones in the Liver, Ducts, or Gall Bladder, then it is evident it muft be difpofed to Lentors prior to its hardening into ftone.

Let the Bile run into Lentors from any caufe, fuch as a fedentary life, and in confequence a want of due vibration of the Liver and its appendages; then if it run into Lentors within the pores or in the Hepatick Duct, and a ftone formed in thefe parts, or Cyft, or its duct, by fome vibration of the parts, or other motion, by riding, falling, vomiting, or paffions of the Mind, be thrown out of the Liver or Cyft, or ducts of either, into the common duct, then will a jaundice commence, attended with white ftools: and if the obftruction perfift, the Blood will become fo faturate with bile, even to blacknefs, that neither will the Heart uniformly move, nor will the fecretions

tions be in proportion to the food, nor
to one another, nor will the Lymph
vitally unite with the Fibres; but the
whole fyftem, as from an internal fuppuration or other foul irritating matter,
having no Gland to fecern it, will go
to confufion, and terminate in death.
And the fame may be argued if any
immoveable tumor of a neighbouring
part fhould prefs the common Duct,
or a fwelling of its own Tunics or the
Tunic of the Inteftines through which
it paffes, or a preffure on the Orifice
within the Inteftine, which cannot be
removed.

But if a Lentor or Stone in one or
more Ducts within the Liver or Hepatick Duct perfift there, then will the
bile return to the Cava, and tinge the
Serum, and produce the fymptoms of
pale yellow fkin, and urine of a deeper
yellow; and if the Lentor or Stone does
not wholly conftipate the Hepatick
Duct, the bile paffing the unobftructed
Ducts in the Liver, and between the
Stone or Lentor and the Tunics of the
Duct,

Duct, will conserve the stools of a
yellow colour; or should there be a total obstruction of the Hepatick Duct,
the stools will be coloured by the cyftick bile as long as the bile lasts therein,
if it receives all its bile by the cyftick
duct; and even during the whole time
of the jaundice if it receive its bile
from the Liver directly, through its
Tunics *.

But should there be several stones
in the Ducts of the Liver or Cyft, which
pass off into the Inteftine, in some time
after their falling into the common
Duct; then will the jaundice, if the
Duct be totally conftipated for the
time, be attended with white stools;
but as the stone falls into the inteftine
it will intermit, and be attended at the
time with a loosenefs of yellow stools,
and return again when another defcends;
but if the stones be not so large as wholly
to conftipate the Duct, then in the time
of the jaundice, as when it intermits, will

* Drake's Anthropologia V. 1. 102.

the

the ſtools be yellow. Again, if the Ducts in the Liver be agitated with a Spaſm, or the Hepatick or common Duct, as from any affection of the Mind, or by conſent with ſome nervous Membrane, as the Skin or Inteſtine, or with the irritation of the bile itſelf, too ſharp for the Ducts, the bile will return to the Blood and affect the jaundice ; but as theſe cauſes are not of duration, the bile, when the Ducts are in diaſtole, will fall into the Inteſtines, and colour their contents, and the jaundice will be of a ſhort duration, like the cauſes which produced it.

But as to that ſort of jaundice which is ſometimes obſerved to ariſe from ſtones in the Gall Bladder, the following obſervation may contribute ſomething towards a more exact knowledge of the nature of this diſtemper and effects than I have found it.

O B-

OBSERVATION III.

Symptoms and Effects of the Stone in the Gall Bladder.

Mrs. Bolton was forty years old, had led a very sedentary life, and was troubled with repeated fits of the jaundice, which wore away and returned at uncertain periods; and was ever liable, as well about the times of the jaundice as at other times, to pains in the lower Belly. On the 23d of April 1756, she was seized with a violent pain near the pit of the Stomach, and retraction of the part toward the Spine, and a strong vomiting; the pain was propagated acutely from the pit of the Stomach in the direction of the Gall Bladder to the Back, but without any quickness of the pulse or other febrile appearance; the fit was eased, and afterward entirely removed by the Thebaic Tincture. On the first of January the following year, the pain and other symptoms returned in the same place, with an intumescence seemingly in the Musculi Recti, near

the

the Navel, and without fever as before.
About the fourth of the fame month it
wore off by degrees, and the ufe of the
fame tincture ; but there immediately
fucceeded a quick pulfe or flow fever,
attended with purulent urine, and deep
fweats ; and on the feventh of June following, a ftrong loofenefs fupervening,
fhe died.

The body by her particular defire
being the next day opened by Mr.
Ruxton and Lifter, we found in the
center of the Liver, which was otherwife very well conftituted, an apoftem
of the fize of a pullet's egg, of very
well digefted pus ; the Colon underneath the Liver was denigrated for a
hand's breadth, and the Fibres of its
external Tunic rent afunder.　In the
Gall Bladder there was two ftones, one
of the fize of a nutmeg, and the other
lefs ; we faw nothing preternatural in
the Ducts or elfewhere in this Venter ;
the Lungs were livid, with tubercles
here and there, which being cut with
the apex of the knife, emitted innumerable

merable drops of well digested pus, which had infiltrated into the Interstices of the Veffels, from the Blood being therewith faturated by the reflux of the pus from the Liver.

Now as the flow fever was confquent only of the laft fit, and as fuch fevers arife from internal fuppurations tainting the Blood, we may conclude the formation of the apoftem recent, which was even manifeft from its appearance only; but the violent pain immediately preceded, and was tranfverfe through the Colon and Liver; and pain being the uneafinefs which attends the idea of continuity folving, we may fafely affirm that the formation of the apoftem was owing to a rupture of the Fibres of the Liver, and an extravafation in confequence, and the more efpecially as the Fibres of the Colon were evidently rent. It was owing therefore to fpafms of the Liver that its Fibres were folved, and let the Blood extravafate; and to the like fpafms that the Tunics of the Colon were rent and gangrened. But if any man fhould fay, how can a gangrene arife from a fpafm? Let it be confidered that a fpafm will not only extravafate the Blood into the Inteftines of the Veffels of any part, but the Fibres by being ftretched lofe their elafticity, and fuffer the extravafate Blood to reft there, and the circulation in the part being totally fufpended, the part muft evidently die.

Again, as we obferve that a ftone in the Kidney being diflodged from its ufual place of eafy refidence,

dence, and either so turned in the Kidney or its Pelvis, or having fallen into the Ureter with the flux of urine in the Diastole of the Ureter, will draw not only the Kidney, but Ureter, Bladder, Stomach, and Intestines into very painful spasms; so one or more stones in the Gall Bladder may, by mutation of place, either in the Bladder or its Neck, or Cystick Duct, from some extraordinary motion or vibration of the Gall Bladder or its Ducts, draw the Liver and its Ducts, Colon, and Stomach, into such spasms as may not only return the Hepatick Bile into the Cava for the present, but by that extreme tension solve the union of the Fibres of one part, and rend and gangrene the Membrane in another.

We may further observe, that a swelling in a Muscle may arise from a spasm by extravasating the blood into the Interstices of its Vessels, or by forcing and conserving more Blood therein than it has when uninfluenced by disturbing causes.

And yet further that pains in a part without a fever may be held sometimes to arise from spasms of the Fibres, rather than quantity, quality, or motion of the contents of the part.

As to the treatment of the person where there is reason to suspect stones (for there are often many stones in the Gall Bladder and Ducts, as there are in the Kidnies, without signifying themselves either by jaundice or pain) reason tells us that it ought to be nearly the same where we have reason to think there are stones in the Kidnies. A dissolvent for a cystick stone, if we had one, would be much less likely to succeed here than in the Kidnies, by reason

of

of the difproportion of Blood and urine flowing through the Kidnies, and the Blood and Bile paffing through the Cyft; for as to diffolve a ftone in the Kidney, Ureter, or Bladder, the Blood and Urine muft be fo changed that they fhall be a menftruum for the ftone, fo the Blood and Bile of the Cyft muft be fo changed as to be a menftruum for the cyftick ftone. However, until this matter be fettled by trial and experience, it may be of ufe to keep the Colon pretty free of contents, left the preffure fhould caufe any effort of the Gall Bladder which fhould bring on a fit: Abftinence from exceffive feeding, fpirituous liquors, and violent exercife, may contribute to the fame effect.

And laftly we may note, that a free communication with the external air is neither neceffary to the putrefaction or irritable quality of the extravafated Blood.

But fhould this reafoning be erroneous, we may at leaft affirm that inflammation and its confequences, apoftem and gangrene, may be caufed by ftones in the Gall Bladder; yet if it was an inflammation, then fuch can be affected without a quicknefs in the pulfe.

OBSERVATION IV.

Vomiting from an Induration of the Pancreas.

A man about forty, of a middle fize, was taken into Stevens's in March 1756.

F   He

He complained of a ficknefs at Stomach, a vomiting after meals, and in confequence a coftivenefs; in fome time after his coming to the houfe a tumour appeared in Epigaftrio, the tumour was hard, and when preffed with the hand exhibited the fenfe of a full pulfation, correfponding to the pulfe in the Wrift. The tumour increafing brought on an inceffant vomiting when he took any food, and fo a general marafmus, and death on the eighth of June following.

In the Cavity of the Cheft every thing was right. In the lower Belly the Inteftines were black, and chiefly the fmall ones; underneath the Stomach and Colon a tumour appeared, the fmall Inteftines being removed, it reached from the Duodenum to the left fide of the Stomach, Spleen, and Kidney, to all which it firmly adhered, particularly to the pofterior part of the Stomach, which was likewife indurated, and rent in the feparation of it from the tumified part: Now the Stomach

mach and Colon being carefully removed from about the tumour, it appeared an indurated Pancreas diffused
from the Liver through the whole Epigaftrum to the Spleen; and the Gall
Bladder was extended to three times
its natural fize.

A permanent ficknefs at Stomach therefore, a
vomiting after meals, a hard fwelling arifing in the
Epigaftrum, attended with a pulfe correfponding to
the Pulfe in the Wrift, may fometimes fignify an
intumified and indurated pancreas.

It appears too that parts difeafed communicate
their ill difpofitions to each other, and efpecially to
thofe nearly in contact with them, and fo the Dura
Mater being inflamed and ulcerated, will adhere to
and ulcerate the Pia Mater, the Membrane of the
Lungs will infect the Pleura, of the Liver and
Spleen the Diaphragm, and fo on; and indeed I
have obferved even an apoftem of the Lungs arife from
a large fuppuration in the Loins; the naufea and vomitings were caufed by the diftemper of the Stomach derived from the pancreas; the pulfation felt
at the pit of the Stomach was very probably propagated through the denfe and indurated body from
the Aorta, on which this vifcus immediately refts;
and this laft fymptom is ftronger for the exiftence
or induration of fomething between the Trunk of
the Aorta and Integuments than any other; for if
the parts above the Aorta are foft and pliable, the

Pulfe

Pulse is lost in the Membranes, nor can it be perceived unless in very emaciated bodies, wherein I have felt the Pulse of the Aorta as clear as in the Wrist, and the same too has been observed by Galen *. And it is rather indicant of an induration of the Pancreas than any other part, for this reason, that being a Gland † constituted of a convolution of Arteries and Veins, it is more liable thereby to obstructions and swellings than the Membranes about it whose Vessels are more rectilineal.

The enlargement of the Gall Bladder was owing to the pressure of the tumour on the common Duct of the Liver and Bladder, or the Duodenum, from whence we may make some estimate of the intensity of the power with which the Bile is expressed from the Liver, either immediately through the Tunics of the Cyst, or by the mediation of the hepatick and cystic Ducts into the Bladder, or that in the Diastole of the Cyst, it receives Bile, which not being able to emit, it enlarges, as the Bladder of urine does, or the Ureters, or any Artery or Vein will, when unable to express their contents.

We may note by the way too that a pressure on the common Duct able to expand the Cyst was unable here to force back the Bile through the Liver into the branches of the Cava; moreover if the Cyst is filled directly from the Liver, the Ducts either must have Valves, as the Thoracic Duct has at its exit in the Subclavian, or pass oblique through the Tunics of the Cyst, as the Ureters do in their route through

---

* In Introduct. in Pulsum, & de dignoscend. Pulf.
† Idem de Meth. medendi, l. 13.

the

the Membranes of the Bladder of Urine, or elfe there muſt have been a great accumulation of Bile in the branches of the Pores, or a black jaundice if the Cyſt communicate with the branches of the Porta in the Liver directly, inaſmuch as the Bile of the Cyſt is blacker than the Bile of the Pores.

As to the treatment of the Perſon where there is reaſon to ſuſpect an induration and enlargement of this Viſcus, ſhould the Stomach be unable to bear medicines intended to clear the Inteſtine, the exhibition of laxative Clyſters, ſuch as a weak infuſion of ſenna, with lenitive electuary, and oil, will, by removing the contents of the Colon, take off the preſſure from the tumour, whereby the motion of the Blood through the Aorta and Cava will be more uniform, and the anxiety conſequent of the inequality of motion through theſe Veſſels thereby remitted, if not totally removed for the preſent; which probably will give opportunity to exhibit broths or other nouriſhment by ſpoonfuls to keep up the powers of the ſyſtem, until by the increment of the tumour, the motion of the Aorta, and in conſequence the heart, ſhall end in confuſion, and the ſyſtem itſelf in putrefaction and death.

I ſaid above that I had obſerved an apoſtem of the Lungs conſequent of another in the Loins; the following obſervation will illuſtrate the truth of the affirmation.

O B S E R V A T I O N V.

Abscess in the Lungs from another in the Loins.

Mistress Graham in her thirtieth year, and in the seventh month of her pregnancy, fell down stairs, and hit herself in the fall on the left Loin, a little above the Ilium, against the edge of one of the stairs; her stays preserved the integuments from contusion, but the whole force of the blow being transmitted to the Spine, the contused flesh being neglected, did there impostumate. From the time she lay in about the end of December 1758, her left thigh became useless and swelled, and an exceeding great pain was propagated from the Ilium, in the direction of the Psoas Muscle, through the Groin, and along the Iliac vessels and nerves, which was attended with a slow fever. On the eighteenth of February 1759, a large soft intumescence appeared in the Loin above

above the Ilium: On the twenty-fixth a Diarrhœa fupervening, the tumor decreafed, another appearing in the Groin. The fourth of March the Potential Cautery was applied to the Loin: On the fifth the Efchar being pierced, about **three pints of a** purulent colluvies were drawn off; the fever fubfifted. **On** the fourteenth the flux from the Loins ftopping, the Groin, which had fubfided fince the fifth, again fwelled: On the fixteenth, **from** a violent paffion of anger, **the tumor in the Groin** difappeared. The feventeenth a total fuppreffion of Urine, attended with an Intumefcence of the Hypogaftrium. The eighteenth a copious flux of Urine coming **on,** it again fubfided, the fever fubfifting with great pain and fwelling and immobility of the Thigh, a troublefome cough, loofenefs, and wafting. On the fixth of April fhe died.

On opening the Body the next day, we found the urinary Bladder moderately diftended with Urine; from the **Spine along** the Pfoas Mufcle and Iliac

F 4   Veffels

Veſſels into the Groin and Thigh, the
whole ſpace was inundated with Pus.
In the left ſide of the Lungs too was
a very large abſceſs covered by the
Pleura, to which the Lungs ſtrictly adhered.

Now ſince Mrs. Graham before the fall was not
unhealthy, we may reaſonably ſay, the formation of
this pulmonary abſceſs commenced ſince the ſuppu-
ration at the Loins, and derived its origin from it ; but
as the Blood, ſaturate with the pus flowing through the
irritable Membrane of the air pipe, occaſioned the
cough, throw the irritable Membranes of the Inteſtines the Diarrhœa, and through the ventricles of the
Heart the fever or quickneſs of the pulſe, ſo did it
death which terminates the whole ; foraſmuch as when
the Blood is ſaturate with heterogeneous materials, and
there be no gland to ſecern it, neither will it aſſimi-
late the food, nor vitally unite with the Fibres, nor
animate the Syſtem.

And it appears moreover that an apoſtem and
irritable pus may be formed deep in the Muſcles,
and from an external cauſe, without free communication with the external air.

SECT.

SECT. IV.

Of the DROPSY.

OBSERVATION I.

Anasarca from an Uterine Hæmorrhage.

A Woman about fifty came to Stevens's in May 1752. Six months before, she had the catamenia for the last time, and the flooding continuing some months; first her legs swelled, and in succession the whole system of the Muscles, and she died the latter end of the same month. In October the same year another of thirty-eight, in Stevens's, had an Uterine Hæmorrhage continuing for a year; first her legs swelled, then an ascites succeeded.

Women

Women are therefore liable to fall into dropfies
from an uterine hæmorrhage, and that near the time
of the termination of the Catamenia chiefly.

In great loffes of Blood, whether from the Lungs,
as in obfervation 6, Sect. 2, or from the uterus, as
in thefe, by the emptinefs of the veffels, and confequent lofs of motion in the Fibres, fanguification is
fo far enfeebled, that the fluid in the veffels is moftly
an ill concocted Serum, whofe particles are but loofely
connected, which by the rarity of the veffels from a
defect of blood in their Tunics, and want of vivid
motion in the fecretory organs to drain off the abundance, and want of motion in the Heart to throw
it round by the veins; it refts in the veins firft and
then tranfudes, either into the interftices of the Mufcles or Cavities ; for when the veffels are filled with
healthy Blood, enriched with Spirits, the motion
of the Heart, Veffels, and Secretions will be much
more vivid, and the Tunics of the Veffels denfer ;
for the Heart and Fibres owe not only their nou-
rifhment but their motion to the Blood.

Again, from weaknefs of Sanguification the poor
effect of Lymph appofited to the Fibres is neither af-
fimilate nor vitally united, nor yet thrown off from
the Fibres, fo that by new acceffion of Lymph, and
diffufion of it over the Fibres, it at length drips
thence into the interftices of the Mufcles, and effects
that fort of dropfy termed Anafarca, which it may
alfo do in the Membranes within and effect a dropfy
of the Cavities ; and thus we may conceive how a
dropfy arifes from Hæmorrhages and weaknefs of
Sanguification, and nutrition in confequence.

O B-

OBSERVATION II.

Anasarca from Obstruction in the Skin.

In spring **1753**, a young woman about twenty came to St. George's, in London: she had taken cold by travelling in a coach from York to London about three weeks before, and had not only the Catamenia stopped, but became universally anasarcous. Evacuations artificial relieved her sometimes; but she was taken with a strong loofeness about two months after, which continuing three days, she was thereby cured.

The Skin therefore, by being obstructed from cold, may turn away the course of secretion from the surface of the Body; and if the confined Lymph be not drawn off by the Kidnies, or other secretory organ, it may transude into the cellular Membrane of the Muscles, and fill their Interstices universally.

A strong Diarrhœa coming on, a Leucophlegmatia cures it*. That is, the vessels of the parts will

---

* Hip. Aph. et lib. de diebus judicatoris et Coacæ prænotiones.

some-

fometimes abforb extravafated Lymph, and tranf-
fer it to another part, and there excern it.

We may likewife obferve too, that the fulnefs of
the veffels and the change induced in their motions, may by its action on the Uterus ftop the Catamenia.

OBSERVATION III.

Afcites from obftructions in the Skin.

In Auguft **1752**, a cooper came to
Stevens's, who from colds by working
in the open air, had not only an anafarcous dropfy, but even an afcites.

And I obferved the fame in a brick-
layer at the fame time.

An afcites therefore as well as an anafarcous
dropfy, may arife from the antecedent caufes of colds,
or ftop to perfpiration from the Skin. That is, the
confined Serum may exfude as well from the Membrane of the Cavity as the Cellular Membrane of the
Mufcles; for as we obferve fuch copious exhala-
tions from the Skin in violent exercife, or ftrong and
inceffant labour, which by condenfing puts on the
form of fweat; fo may we eafily conceive, that if
the exhalation is confined in the Skin, and the rarefaction and vapours arifing from the Blood ftill continue, that the vapour afcending from the Blood
may

may find a vent from the internal Membranes, and
by there condenfing produce a dropfy of the Cavity,
or by fwelling the ferous veffels of this Venter to a
Diairefis.

OBSERVATION IV.

Afcites from Obftructions in the Kidnies.

A boy about thirteen, in St. George's
in London 1753, had fuppreffions of
urine, and being fearched with the
catheter, no ftone was perceived. He
had been cut for the ftone, and one
extracted from the Bladder two years
before; but the fymptoms of fuppreffion
and pains in the Loins, chiefly the left,
toward which he was fomewhat incurvated, perfifting, attended too with an
urinous vapour, exhaling from and
moiftening the Skin, he fell at length
into a dropfy of the Belly.

From the continuance of the fymptoms after operation, and the urinous humidity ever exhaling from
the Skin, it is more than probable that one if not
both Kidnies were infarcted with fand, gravel, or
ftone. And as this dropfy came long after operation, from which he was very well recovered, we
may

may fay that an Afcites may arife fometimes from obftruction to the fecretion of urine.

And that the quantity ftopped in the Veffels from feparation, by the Kidnies being infarcted, will in time caufe an accumulation fufficient for the purpofe, even though a great part of what ought to be drawn off by urine exhale in the fkin; we may gather from the rules of Sanctorius, Keil, and Robinfon, if the quantity of drink is given for a time; and the like may be argued of a fuppreffion of fecretion by the Skin.

OBSERVATION V.

Afcites from Obftructions in the Liver.

In March 1752 a girl about fixteen was taken in at Stevens's, who had a tumour below the Cartilage of the Sternum, nearly midway between the Hypochonders, rather inclining to the right, attended with a dropfy afcites; it pointed after fome time, and was livid at the apex, and feemed like an abfcefs from an inflammation. Emollient and warm cataplafms being applied, it broke in a few days, and above three pints of hydatids came from the orifice at times, and fome alfo by the

Rectum

Rectum. In a few weeks after she was discharged well of her ulcer and dropsy, but with some degree of jaundice, appearing only in the Tunica albuginea of the eyes.

Now as it is a known property of the Liver to be liable to such obstructions as generate hydatids, it is very probable her dropsy took origin from this tumour existent in the Liver; for if the Vein termed Porta is pressed by any cause, the Mesentery, Intestines, and Spleen being thereby swelled, their Vessels will be rarer at their terminations in the Membranes than they were before, and will thereby be the more disposed to let their Lymph transude in the manner of Diapedesis; or if there are serous Vessels in these Membranes, not admitting red globules of Blood, more Lymph may be turned into these Vessels than their tender Tunics can bear, so that it may transude as by Diapedesis, or by the way of Diœresis let their Lymph fall into the Cavity; and the same may arise by a pressure on the branches of the Cava in the Liver, by which the Membranes of the Viscus may be given to swell. But the Hydatids with their contents, by the adherence of the Liver to the Peritoneum, and suppuration of the Membrane and parts above it, finding an exit from within the Liver, suffered the Blood to go on more freely throughout the unobstructed part of the Viscus, and so the swelling of the Spleen, Intestines, and Mesentery subsiding, the extravasation stopped,

and

I.

and that which had formerly leaked was again abforbed, leaving however fome degree of preffure on
the Biliary Ducts, which returning the Bile to the
Cava tinged the Serum, and caufed that flight appearance of jaundice which remained ; and I the rather take this to be the mode of effection, for the
rupture of the Hydatids would probably afford too
fmall a quantity of water to make an afcites vifible.

And it appears too that though a Liver enlarged
by unequal nutrition, which is only the affection of
its Fibres, or fwelled by too much Blood or cold
congeftions in the Porta, will not of neceffity produce a jaundice, yet a tumor may be of fuch a fort
and fituation in this Vifcus as to effect it fometimes.

But fometimes too obftructions in the Liver, of
another kind than thofe which raife Hydatids, or
rather a peculiar fort of tumors, by their preffure on
the branches of the Porta, differing in fpecies from
the former, may caufe a dropfy of the Belly, I
had an oportunity of feeing, while I was reviewing
thefe obfervations.

O B S E R V A T I O N VI.

A boy of fourteen came to Mercer's * in Auguft, with an immenfe afcites, for which he had been repeatedly

---

* Regifter of caufes at Mercer's for 1762.

tapped ;

tapped; but the water ftill tranfuding, he died on the 10th of September 1762.

In the Lower Belly we found the Liver wholly conftituted of little firm globules, quite folid to fenfe, corre-fponding to the defcription of Marcel-lus, Malpighius*, or like the vitella-rium in a laying hen †, except that thefe globules were among themfelves more near in a proportion of equality than thofe of the vitellarium are. This Liver however weighed but one pound fifteen ounces Troy, and the Spleen one pound ten ounces.

Now though Malpighius defcribes his Liver as a conglomerate Gland, yet the injections of Rufchius and other anatomifts have put it out of difpute, that Malpighius's Livers were morbid, or their ftruc-ture preternatural ; and as the Spleen in no wife dif-fered from a ftate of nature but weight, at leaft as to fenfe, we may fafely conclude that the preffure of thefe little bodies on the branches of the Veins in the Liver, were the immediate caufe effective of the leakage.   And indeed the largenefs of Spleen would incline one to think, that from the flower motion of the Blood in that Vifcus, by reafon of its obftruction

---

* De Hepate, c. 3.   † Hervey de gen. an. excer. 3.

G   in

in the Liver, the Spleen, by unequal nourishment, had outgrown its ordinary size and just proportion to the Liver.

And universally I believe from the various and great impediments the Blood meets in its transit through the Membranes of the Lower Belly, it comes that dropsies are more frequently observed in this venter than in the two superior.

But as to the above subject, there was nothing of morbid disposition or ill conformation to be seen in any other part of the lower or middle Venter, and we may affirm the same of the upper Venter, from his preserving a state and powers of understanding and lively voluntary motion, even to the hour of his death.

But obstructions likewise in the Liver will, for the reasons assigned, extravasate Lymph, and even Blood, into the Cavity of the Intestines; and these extravasations are attended with scarce any uneasiness, but that of an obscure pain and weight in the right Hypochondrium, and even sometimes none at all; but a very great and repeated dejection of mind and faintness. And indeed these fluxes, compared with antecedent causes, are no mean argument of such obstructions existing in the Liver. I once myself observed one who, from an anxious solitary life, took to drinking distilled spirits by way of refreshment or dissipation of care, and was turned of fifty, and often jaundiced; that these fluxes returning at uncertain periods relieved her greatly from that load and oppression she complained of before the ejection of the Blood. Now seeing that distilled

spirits are known to infpiſſate the Blood, and fo
conſtrict the Fibres for the prefent, that they are
weaker fometime after a dram *, and that infpiſ-
fated blood will rather be given to ſtop in the Liver than any other part, forafmuch as this bowel,
though its Vein be denfer and ſtronger † than even
the Cava and Aorta, yet as wanting elaſticity to
give its Blood the Arterial Jet, the progrefs of the
Blood will be flower, and obſtructions more likely
to be formed herein, and efpecially as the Blood
returning from the Inteſtines ‡ after depofiting its
phlegm there, as alfo after its Serum is drained off
in a good meafure by the Kidnies, is more infpiſ-
fated than that which paſſes in other parts, even in
a ſtate of texture agreeable to nature, and totally
uninfluenced by the admixture of coagulating medicines; and if the Blood be accumulated in the
Membranes of the Lower Belly, by reaſon of an
obſtruction in the Liver, we need not be furprifed
at the great dejection of mind and faintnefs which
attends, the Heart being thereby deficient of its due
quantity of Blood, which Blood gradually accumulated, being thus extravafated, the Veſſels of the Mefentery are again at freedom to renew their vibrations, and forward the Blood they receive from the
branches of the Celiacs through the part of the
Liver remaining unobſtructed.

It having been an opinion of fome, that the Bile
in a jaundice returning to the Blood does by its fa-
ponaceous quality thin it, and caufe it thereby to

---

* Hales's Hæmoſticks, Exp 15.   † Clifton Winring-
ham, Exp. 47. Lond. 1740.   ‡ Gliſſon anat. Hep. c. 41.

be

be more liable to exfude from the Membranes, which though one would not totally deny, yet feeing that this quality of the human Bile has not been fettled by fufficient experience, I had rather fay that, that ftate of the Liver which returns the Bile does, by obftruction and loading the Membranes, give occafion for the more ready exfudance of the finer part of the Lymph. For if the Pores in the Liver are tumid with Bile they will prefs the branches of the Porta, and by conftant perfeverance, will infenfibly fill the Membranes of the Belly to an exfudance of their Lymph. Laftly, if artificial foaps have fimilar powers with the natural, thofe who take foap pills even to an ounce in the day, for concretions in the urinary parts, fhould be liable to the dropfy, which is oppofite to experience.

OBSERVATION VII.

Afcites from an obftructed Spleen.

In October 1752, a woman about thirty-five was brought to Stevens with an immenfe afcites. Seven years before this fhe received a bruife in the left Hypochondrium. In fome time from the accident the dropfy became fenfible and afterwards encreafed. She was tapped in the hofpital, and five gallons of of water drawn off by the trochar, when an immenfe fpleen prefented itfelf, filling the whole Hypochondrium. A little before her coming to the hofpital, by a fright, fhe was taken with a vomiting of Blood, but not very great in quantity, nor of long continuance. I obferved likewife here that ftate of mental confidence noted by Areteus and Mead.

If obftructions and fwellings of the fpleen arife from others in the Liver, it is no very difficult matter to conceive the manner in which a dropfy of the Belly may be thus effected ; for if the motion is impeded in the Splenick Vein, as it is when the Liver is obftructed, the fpleen and its Membrane will infenfibly fill, and fo the Lymph may exfude : Or by filling the Lymphaticks with more Lymph than their tender Tunics are able to fupport without ex. fudance or rupture. But in obftructions of the fpleen, independent of the Liver, fuch as may arife from a diftemper of the fpleen itfelf, it is not fo eafy to make it out clearly. An ulcer exiftent in the Tunic may partly, by erofion of the Tunic, not fo great as to let the red Globules pafs, and partly by the irritation of its Ichor inciting an afflux of Serum that way, drip fo for a long feries of time, as to fill the cavity of the Belly, which can be rea-

dily

dily known by computing the number of drops an ulcer may be conceived to let fall in a given time.

But in this cafe, where the fwelling of the fpleen was exceeding great, it is probable the Blood extravafated therein by the bruife, did fo by its preffure on the Veins change the progreffion of the Blood in the Arteries of the Vifcus, that the Blood conftantly diffufed through its Membrane fwelled it, or the Membranes of the Stomach, to an exfudance of their Lymph, at every fyftole of the Vifcus; fo that we may fay *de facto*, that a dropfy of the Belly was concomitant with a fwelled and obftructed Spleen, and by reafon that it had its origin from it. I feem alfo to gather that vomiting of Blood may be caufed by the fame indifpofition; for in the paffion of fudden fear, the Blood being hurried to the Spleen and not finding an exit there with eafe and freedom, it returned to the Stomach and there extravafated. And we may alfo note, that the Arteries not only fuffer their Lymph to exfude into the Stomach when its Membranes are loaded, but even red blood through their orifices opening to the Cavity when expanded. I fay the Arteries; for had the vomiting of Blood been concomitant with obftructions of the Liver, the Hæmorrhage would have come from the Veins of the Stomach, ending in the Splenick Vein; as it happened to Mrs. Hudfon, a relation of mine, who died of a jaundice and dropfy, ending at length with an inceffant vomiting of Blood.

In the general reflection of the firft fection we fhewed, from the authority of Webfer, the poffibility

of

of water extravafating in the Head and Spine, together with its antecedent caufes, fymptoms, and effects; and we feemed to think this water fweated from the weak Membrane lining the Ventricles, or from the Membranes about the Brain, or exhaled therefrom, and then condenfed into the form of water, by reafon that fuch obftructions of or preffure on the Veins defcending from the Head, would fwell up the Membranes or vafcular part of the Brain too fuddenly, and be vifible by its effects on the medullary tracts, before the Lymph could collect in any fenfible quantity, unlefs the preffure or obftruction were lefs than any affignable one, and perfifted for a long time; fo that the whole contents of the Skull, by the diffufion of the Lymph, fhould at length become fo humid as to diftill part of that humidity from the moift Membranes.

And we may alfo infer, that a rupture of one or more Lymphaticks (if there be fuch) would fuddenly drown the Brain, as it poffibly did in the cafe of Chriftopher Weiler, recited by Bruner.

And further, that an ulcer exiftent in thefe Membranes would fhew itfelf by convulfive motions in the fyftem of the Mufcles by its irritation, before it would fill the interftices of the Membranes or Ventricles; and that thefe reafons may be transferred to the Membranes and cinericious parts of the Spinal Marrow. And as the preffure on the Veins of the Omentum and Gut ftrangled in an Hernia fills the fack with water, fo in the third fection tranfudation from preffure in fome Veins of the Cheft has been fhewn from reafon to be a poffible caufe of a dropfy

G 4 here;

here; and we may say from reason too, that obstructions in the Veins of the Intercostals returning to the Azygos and Auricle, may fill the Tunics of the same Veins near their origins in the Membranes, and have the same effect; though these Veins are portions of cones, whose angles at the vertex are exceedingly acute, yet may, like the Pulmonary Veins, be susceptible of obstruction; and all this [in the mode of extravasation by Diapedesis.

Moreover we shewed, from observation and reason, that an ill cured pleurisy leaving distempered Membranes produced it also, either by dripping their Ichor, or pressing of their tumor on some Vein of the Chest : And this by the mode of Diæresis and Diapedesis.

And we also infer from the authority of Cooper, that a dropsy of the Chest may be concomitant with, and by reason did arise from, obstructions in the Kidneys; for he tells us * that on opening the Body of an elderly gentleman who died of an asthma from water in the Chest, that the right Kidney was but a third of its natural size, and that too with large Hydatids on its surface; the left Kidney also lessened, but not so much as the right, and its ureter almost impervious from its petrification : And the mitral Valves of the left Ventricle petrified in several places also, so that we may say the system, loaded with Serosities, suffered part thereof to exsude from the internal Membranes; and rather from those of the Chest, by reason the petrification of the Valves

* Transf Phil. V. 5. p. 240.

af

of the Ventricle hindering the uniform egrefs of the Blood from the Lungs, its Membrane was thereby more tumid with Lymph than it otherwife would be: And the fame may be argued of a polypous Concretion in the pulmonary Vein. And we alfo fhewed that a dropfy of the Pericardium was concomitant with, and probably arofe from, a permanent obftruction of the Lungs.

And we likewife conclude by reafon, that if there are Lymphaticks in the human Cheft, that by their continuity folved from quantity, quality, or unequal motion of their Lymph, or by Diapedefis from their extended Tunics, the fame may arife.

In the fixth obfervation of the fecond fection, we likewife proved, by mere obfervations, that a dropfy of the Mufcles, termed Anafarca, did arife from a great depletion of the Blood from the Lungs and Arm. And in the preceding obfervations we faw that not only an anafarcous dropfy but even an Afcites, followed profufe Hemorrhages from the Uterus, together with the mode by which it was effected; and that both forts are caufed by obftructions in the Skin; and that an afcites is caufed by obftructions in the Kidnies and Liver *, the former by filling the whole fyftem, and the latter by filling the Membranes of the Lower Belly with Lymph; and that an afcites was concomitant with, and very probably arofe from, obftructions and diftempers of the fpleen, and fuch are fome of the material caufes of dropfies. Moreover, if there are Lymphaticks in this

* Galen de locis affectis, lib. 5, C, 7.

Venter

Venter of the human Subject, we may say, as in a
dropsy of the Cheft, that by obstruction to its uniform motion, or continuity solved from the quantity
or quality of their Lymph, a dropsy of this cavity
may be effected.

Among the antecedent causes of water congesting
in the Cavities then, we have assigned want of due
secretions by an inert life, or disproportion of fluid
to solid food, and quantity of both too great for the
powers, by which the whole System is turgid with
Lymph, which flowing through weak Membranes,
does by expanding dispose them to leak : But I argue
further, that it is possible the passions of the Mind
may antecede and be effective of a dropsy of either
Cheft and Belly, if the Heart and Veffels be agitated
with Spasms, as we often see in the passions of shame,
fear, joy, surprize, and sudden grief. If these passions persevere, or return ever and anon, then will
the left Ventricle by its tremulous motion return the
Blood as often into the Lungs, which in their Syftole
may express the Lymph into the cavities, and by
repetitions of it cause even a notable congestion ; and
if the right Ventricle be often agitated by the same
disturbing causes, the Blood will return through the
Liver, and expand its Membrane, as also all the Membranes of the Lower Belly : But I only mention this
as a possible effect of these disturbing causes, leaving
it to be either proved or rejected as it shall be found
conformable to experience or not : Nor is it possible
that these extravasations should arise from any repeated disturbances of the Ventricles only, but the
same consequential effects may be caused by like

agita-

agitations of the Diaphragm, at leaſt I ſee no contradiction in it.

If water is ſuffered to reſt extravaſate, it will have
theſe effects, that either growing acrid or putrid, it
will ſcald and corrupt the parts about it, or by congeſtion incommode the functions of the parts which
are near it.   In the Legs it will produce ulcers
tending to gangrene; ſo will it corrupt the Membranes of the Lower Belly.   In the Ventricles of
the Brain it will expand them even to dilate the
Brain to the thickneſs of a Membrane, if the Bones
give way as they do in Hydrocephalous Fœtus's and
Infants *, if not, it compreſſes the medullary tracts,
and ends either in an apoplexy or paralyſis, as the
preſſure is univerſal, or greater on ſome than other
tracts.   If the extravaſation is above the cortical
part, it will preſs it down to a third of the ſpace it
before poſſeſſed.   In the cavity of the Cheſt it will,
by ſucceſſive congeſtion, whether by infiltration or
effuſion, raiſe the ribs firſt, and when the ribs are at
the utmoſt expanſe, preſs the Lungs and Heart, even
to ſuffocation and ſwooning.   If between the In-
tercoſtals and Pleura, that Membrane will be ſeparated
from the Ribs, and preſs the Lungs to the ſame effect, which appears from diſſection; foraſmuch as
when the Sternum has been raiſed and removed,
there at firſt appeared as if there were no ſuch parts
as Heart or Lungs in the Cheſt.   In the Mediaſtinum it will have the ſame impreſſion on the
great veſſels ariſing out of and ending in the Heart.

* Mauriceu de Mul. Morb. lib. 3, c. 28. Paris 1682.

In

In the cavity of the Pericardium it will interrupt
the expansion of the Auricles and Ventricles. In
the cavity of the Lower Belly it will force the Diaphragm up into the Cheft, and by leffening the
fpace of its cavities, bring on a fhortnefs of Breath ;
and preffing the Liver and Kidnies, hinder their natural fecretions, and by preffing the Stomach and
alimentary Canal, the due progreffion of the food
therein : And if it arife and congeft within the
Ovaria, it will extend the Ovary, until preffing the
Illiac Nerves and Veffels, the Hips and Thighs are
tortured with acute pains and fwellings ; and the
Urine by its preffure on the Ureters, if both Ovaria are affected, or even one only, will be cohibited.

Elinor Proudfort, about twenty, in September
1762 came to Mercer's : fhe had an acute pain in
her Hip, which propagated itfelf down the Thigh
and Leg, even to the Ancle : we bled, purged,
bliftered, and applied the plafter in common ufe,
of Burgundy pitch and turpentine, with an eighth
of euphorbium, to little purpofe : In the beginning
of October a large circumfcribed fwelling appeared
in the Illiac region, which infenfibly diffufed itfelf
toward the Spine, and the foregoing Symptoms increafed, even to a lofs of the Limb, with a fuppreffion of the inteftinal and urinal Excretions. In
November fhe left the Hofpital for fear of being
diffected.

Now as there is no part in the Iliac Region fo
liable to a large circumfcribed increafing Tumor as
the Ovarium is, we may fay that an enlargement of
that

that part, whether by increment of Fibres, as in the cafe of unequal nutrition, or by water extravafated into the interftices of its Veffels, effected the œdema of the extremity, and the acute pain and fever concomitant with it.

Tumors of this kind I have obferved to attend abortions, difficult labours, and long retention of the Catamenia, though none of them were incident to Proudfort.

Between the Mufcles and Peritoneum it will have the fame effect as between the Intercoftals and Pleura. If any man fhould fay, how is it poffible that water can extravafate, collect, and act with fuch exceeding preffure ? Let it be confidered that all foft organical parts are ever in a ftate of Syftole and reciprocal Diaftole. If the fine Membrane of the Ventricles or Glands of the Plexus are given to leak in every Diaftole of the Brain, there will be a fpace left to be fupplied by a new diftillation, and the Brain will lofe fo much of its due dimenfion, and in procefs of time the lofs of fpace, though lefs at firft than any given one, will become fenfible, and the fame may be argued of any other part into which the Membranes may be given to exfude. Moreover if the leakage fhould come from the Dura or Pia Mater, the fubfidence of the Brain will allow fpace for fucceffive drops.

That a dropfy of the Head and Spine, or rather the ftate of the parts in the Head and Spine, wherein the Brain and Marrow, and their Membranes, are foaked in ferofities without much congeftion in the Cavities, and which are fignified by the fymptoms

of

of vertigo, drowfinefs, head-achs, and paralyfes, may be fometimes cured by purging frequently re-peated, to invite the Serum to the Inteftines, and by leffening the diet, and chiefly the drink, and perfe-vering therein for many months, we fhewed from the authority of Robinfon and Mead, and other eva-cuations near the part affected, in the general obfer-vation of the firft fection.

That a dropfy of the Cheft, if it arife from mere exfudance, and the Membranes of the Cheft are free from permanent fwellings, ulcers, or ferous ab-fceffes, or other ill difpofitions of the Lungs, may be cured by the powers of the Membranes, I argued by comparing them with the artificial dropfy pro-duced by Mufgrave ; and that it is relieved from any caufe by draining the whole fyftem of its Serum by purging repeatedly ; and the immediate danger put off for a time by the paracentefis.

That a dropfy in the Belly too may be cured by the Membranes refuming the extravafated Lymph, we may infer from the reafons of the celebrated Kaw *, inferring the neceffity of reforbing from the conftancy with which the Membranes exhale ; and it would very probably be proved, if fuch experi-ments as thofe of Mufgrave were made in this Ven-ter, by deductions ftronger than reafon only †. But when a dropfy of the Belly admits of cure by purg-ing, diureticks, and the paracentefis, we may con-clude that the extravafation arofe rather by reafon the whole fyftem was turgid with Lymph, by con-

* Leidæ 1738.   † Sharp on Operations, c. 13. Lond. 1758.

finement

finement of fome fecretion of the Skin or Kidnies, fo
that the ferous Veffels leaked in the mode of diapedefis; but the organs refuming their functions,
the water is either abforbed or drained by fafting or
the other mode of artificial evacuations by irritations
as above; or that it arofe from the inertnefs of
the Liver, by which the Membranes of the Lower
Belly were loaded with Blood, and for want of due
progreffion depofited its Lymph, which probably
was the cafe where the vomits recommended by Sydenham had fuch extraordinary effects; but if a
dropfy of the Belly arife from a fixed obftruction of
the Liver or Spleen, or incurable infarction of the
Kidnies, or ulcers or tumefactions in the Mefentery,
then we muft draw off the water by irritation, and
the paracentefis repeated as neceffity requires; and
the ufe of warm, generous, and fpirituous cordials,
which enliven and fupport the Heart, while the fyftem fhall continue to move.

Laftly, that a dropfy anafarcous may be cured
by the part reforbing the Lymph, we proved precifely in the fecond obfervation of this fection, where
being transferred to the Inteftines it was there extravafated; but an anafarcous dropfy arifing from
mere fullnefs and confequent leakage, is to be treated
by irritation of the Inteftines, and then of the Kidnies, a remarkable inftance of which Sir Richard
Blackmore relates, wherein all the water was driven
off through the Kidnies by chalybeat waters, in an
otherwife infuperable anafarca; and if it arife from
profufe hæmorrhages, the cure by irritation is to be
deferred, till the Veffels are filled with Blood, of fuch
quality,

quality, that the Heart, enabled thereby, may throw
it round through the fyftem of the Veins, in order
to ftop the infiltration, which is done by generous
diet to fupport the powers and keep up the fecretions, and then by diuretics, not too much adding
to the quantity of Lymph ; and laftly, by innumerable punctures of the hydropical parts, which correfpond in proportion to the paracentefis of the Cavities : But care is be taken here that the fections of
the extremities be not too large, efpecially if the
anafarca extend throughout the whole fyftem of the
Mufcles (for in a partial anafarca the danger cannot
be very confiderable) by reafon I have feen more
than once, which has been likewife obferved by Galen * and Mead †, where the incifions being three
or four inches long, the Serum running out too
fuddenly, they have been taken with rigors and
fhudderings, with an immenfe fenfation of coldnefs,
and in two or three days have died fo ; very probably for this, that the preffure being taken off the
Arteries of the Mufcles, left the interior Arteries and
left Ventricle deficient of Blood, and the preffure
being taken off the Veins of the Mufcles, relaxed by
foaking in the Lymph, neither they nor the foftened
Fibres of the Mufcles had elafticity enough to exprefs the load of Blood they were too fuddenly filled
with ; or the Serum extravafed, at once drawn off,
the remainder in the Veffels leaked out after it, and
left the Cruor within too infpiffate for motion, or
the whole fyftem fo empty, that its organical parts
were deftitute of fluid to conferve their motions.

* De Arte med. ad Glauconem, lib. 1.   † Præcept. med.

Should

Should a dropfy anafarcous arife from preffure on the Trunks of the Cavæ, as in a dropfy of the Cheft, or fwelled Ovaria, either by water therein or enlarged in the mode of Sarcofis, then will it be relieved from time to time by draining the Serum through the Inteftines, forcing part thereof through the Kidnies, and Punctures, until the fyftem by the increment of the preffing caufe fhall terminate in death.

But fometimes there are tumors of the Belly having their origin in the Mefentery, and contain a fluid therein, which raife the Integuments and Mufcles of the Belly, and are attended with fymptoms not diffimilar to a dropfy of the Belly ; fo that it might be taken for a tumor effected by extravafated water at large in the Cavity. The undulation of the water in an afcites proper, is readily perceived by placing the palm of one Hand on the fide of the Belly and tapping with the other, but the fluctus of Water encyfted is not fo evident.

OBSERVATION VII.

Elizabeth Flyn, about fourteen, had a tumor gradually increafing in the middle of the Lower Belly for three months, till it came to the fize of an ordinary afcites. The undulation of water was very obfcure, and it was harder than a tumour from water in

H the

the Cavity : Purging relieved her from time to time, but fhe died on the fourth of October laft 1762.

When the Integuments and Mufcles of the Belly were removed, there appeared a tumour among the Inteftines adhering to the Mefentery, and being divided there flowed out a gallon or more of a dilutered fluid ; the Ovarium of the right fide too was larger than a pullet's egg.

Now feeing the Belly may enlarge from fuch different caufes, we ought to be the more circumfpect in tapping, left we leave the perfons worfe than we found them, and difcredit an operation of fervice to mankind when juftly inftituted.

SECT.

SECT. V.

Of the INTESTINES.

DYSENTERIES, like other difeafes, are either epidemical or
acute; the fymptoms of which are a
loofenefs attended with gripes, mucus,
blood in the ftools, and a quick pulfe;
and their immediate caufe, fluxion on
the Inteftines; but they are fometimes
diuturnal, and their immediate caufes
are either habitual fluxion or apoftem.

OBSERVATION I.

*Dyfentery from an Apoftem in the
Rectum.*

A failor about fifty came to Stevens's in October 1756, who for two
years had a dyfentery, contracted at firft
in America; fometimes by the affift-

ance

ance of medicines it ftopped for a
mcnth or two, and then returned; the
loofenefs was not vifcous, bloody, or
watry, nor attended with much pain,
but ftercoral.   At length an ulcer appeared near the Sphincter of the Rectum, and being fearched it was found
to be a compleat fiftula: The operation
for a fiftula being duly performed, and
the part healed, the flux returned no
more.

In that fort of chronical dyfentery then, where
the loofenefs is ftercoral, and without acute pain,
fever, and gripes, we may conceive the caufe to be
rather the Pus or Ichor of an apoftem, fretting the
Inteftine near the place of its exiftence, and propagating its effects through the whole Canal, than
an acrid ferum or humor flowing on, or fecerned
in, the Tunics of the Inteftines; and thefe fymptoms may diftinguifh fometimes whether the caufe
be from fluxion or apoftem; the reafon of which
difference is, the Inteftines are at the fame time fti-
mulated, and their contents diluted with the materials of the fluxion.

Should a dyfentery be caufed by an apoftem
higher in the Tunics of the Rectum, or in the Colon, as it may according to Bartholine * and Hux-
ham †, and the apoftem be recent, the cure will

* Cent. 6, Obf. 2.   † Tranf. Phil. v. 7. 518.

depend on the materials of it being taken into the
habit, and transferred to the Emunctories, or on its
breaking into the Inteftines, that the whole Pus may
be difcharged in ftool; but if the Ichor diftil into
the Cavity of the Inteftine, either conftantly or from
time to time, it will be requifite to fheath the Inteftine from its irritation and corrofive effects by
foft unguents and balfams, fuch as that of Locatellus,
or others of like power, and to clear the Inteftine
repeatedly with lenitive electuary or rhubarb, until
the motions exerted by nature fhall exprefs all the
materials of the apoftem.

The mediate caufes of the iliac paffion are either
fcalding humour flowing in the Membranes of the
Inteftines, or fecerned by their Glands into their
Cavity, or an acrid vapour exhaling therein, whofe
exit has by colds or other antecedent caufes been
confined in the fkin; and thefe caufes have been
difcovered by reafon: obftructions by induration of
their contents; hernias at the Navel [*], Diaphragm [†],
and Groin; and involutions [‡] have been traced by
diffection: But as iliac paffions are acute, and the
Inflammations raifed in the Inteftines moftly terminate by gangrene in a little time when they do not
refolve, fo are they fometimes intermittent, and of
length, and fatal in the end.

[*] Amand. Tranf. Phil. vol. 9. 159.   [†] St. Andre, vol.
5. 267.   [‡] Riverius Cent. 306. 26.

H 3   OBSER-

OBSERVATION II.

Iliac Paſſon from Adherence of the Inteſtines.

In April 1753 came a man from Edinburgh to St. George's hoſpital, who had for three quarters of a year inſufferable pains in the Lower Belly, and ſometimes a vomiting, with a total ſuppreſſion of ſtools and urine. The violence of theſe pains were often allayed by the aſſiſtance of ſtrong purges, the compound powder of ſcammony, with a grain or two of opium, and a clyſter in an hour or ſo, to ſolicit it downward. Sometimes too the torment intermitted of itſelf for a few days, but on the 21ſt of May he was ſeized with a fit of violent pain, in which the day following he died.

On removing the Sternum ſome hard tubercles appeared in the Lungs diſperſedly, but not ſo many or ſo great as to incommode their functions. In the Lower Belly the whole volume of the Inteſtines

Inteftines adhered univerfally, exhibit-
ing the appearance of the Brain when
the Pia Mater is removed ; and their
furfaces, together with the furface of the
Liver, Spleen, and Stomach, were white,
as if fodden in fcalding water ; on the
infide of the Stomach were many fpots
of extravafated Blood, about the fize of
a filver two-pence ; and in the Cavity
of the Belly was a brown liquor diffufed over the furface of the Inteftines ;
there was no other changes evident to
fenfe in the organical conftitution of
any part, nor could it be found whence
the water extravafated.

From the Colour of the Inteftines then, and other
parts in this Venter ; from the inflammatory ftate of
the Stomach, and adherence of the Inteftines, whofe
difpofition it is, in common with other Membranes
in the fyftem, to coalefce from antecedent inflammations ; and from the water found extravafate in
the Cavity, we may fafely infer, that an acrid humour fweated from, or a fcalding vapour expired
from the Membrane of the Cavity, by whofe action
on the Inteftines the accidents related were produced ; for if acrid humours are often generated in the
Blood of fo corrofive a quality, as we obferve in the
humour termed fcrophulous, and others fpecifically

H 4   different,

different, corroding even the bones themfelves, no
wonder then that an humour fimilar in power fhould
raife fuch extreme perception of pain in thefe exqui-
fitely fenfible Membranes, inflame and effect their
unition before they had time to corrode as they do
in parts deftitute of feeling or vifible irritation. So
then we may infer by reafon, that an iliac paffion
may arife from fluxions at firft ; and by diffection,
that the effect of the fluxions may be inflammation
of the Membranes, their union among themfelves,
and confequent obftructions from defect in their
motions, returns of infufferable pain thereby, and
death in the end.

And by the way we may note, that a fuppreffion
of urine may be caufed by the Ureters confenting in
fpafms with the Inteftines, as the Inteftines are known
to do from irritations in the Ureters.

OBSERVATION III.

Iliac Paffion by Involution.

In Auguft 1752, came to Stevens's
a failor from Yarmouth, a little Man,
about twenty-five years old: He had
intolerable pains in the Lower Belly,
which began fix weeks before, and continuing for fome hours, then intermitted. At thefe intervals of pain he re-

3   turned

turned to feed as at other times, but when the Inteftine began to fill, the food ftopped in its paffage below the Navel, and then the torment commenced, and perfifted till, by the affiftance of very ftimulating clyfters, fome ftools were promoted, and thus he was eafier; but thofe means were at length ineffectual, fo the intermiffions being lefs, the pain became almoft continual, and in a violent exacerbation one morning he died, being two months after his arrival at the hofpital.

The Cæcum with its appendicle, and three or four inches of the Ilium, were forced up into the Colon and adhered thereto; and the Colon, rent from its adherence to the Mefentery, lay down in the Pelvis.

Now a little before the commencement of thefe Pains this miferable man had taken very ftrong cathartic pills repeatedly for a virulent gonorrhœa, which wrought him almoft inceffantly.

So then an Iliac Paffion may arife from the involution of one part of the Inteftine into another, from

its

its inflammation and adherence, which obstruct the contents of the Intestine endeavouring to descend, and from the violent and painful Luctus between the Intestine and Obstacle; and this sort of Iliac passion is indicated by the stoppage of the food at a certain place, of which this unhappy man was perfectly sensible.

It appears too, that pain will arise in the Intestines, as well by obstruction of its cavity, as from fluxions on or obstructions in the Vessels of the Membranes, or spasms by affections of their Nerves.

Nor is it dissonant to reason to conclude, these effects took origin from the violent motions of the Intestines raised by the pills; for by the strong actions of the Diaphragm and Muscles of the Belly exerted in intestinal excretions, combined with the motions of the Intestines from the same cause, that such an effect may arise is not very difficult to conceive to one who considers the strength of these motions, and compares them with the experiments of the celebrated Haller *, who by irritation has made introsusceptions in the Intestines of creatures at pleasure, which introsusceptions however, by a series of experiments of the same author, will not produce the Iliac Passions without the inflammation and adherence of their Membranes.

And thus exclusive of the consequences of immoral hernias, swellings of the Testicles, and too

* Opus. parthology Ob. 27, Lusannæ 1755. Tran. Phil. v. 5, 259.

sud-

sudden stoppage of the flux from the Urethra, which are known frequently to follow the repetition of strong cathartic pills of aloe, scammony, and colo quintida, in treating a virulent gonorrhœa we reasonably reduced a possible consequence, worse than the precedent.

OBSERVATION IV.

Suppression of the Contents of the Intestines, from weakness of their Fibres.

Sherman tells us, that Thomas Philips, of Eastthorp in Essex, was very well in every respect till he was a year and a quarter old, and after a loosenefs had such an obstruction of the Intestine, that he did not stool for a fortnight or three weeks together, and from thence it proceeded gradually to an interval of seventeen or eighteen weeks, and continued so till about the age of fifteen, when he re-assumed his natural powers for four or five years; but then the obstructions returned, and continued increasing till he died, even to above twenty weeks interval; and when he did go to stool he evacuated

many

many times a day, and feveral days together, till he had emptied himfelf, the
contents being always thin and foft:
he lived to be near twenty-three years
old, and walked about almoft to the
hour of his death; but his mother
would not permit him to be opened:
And Cooper in his annotations on this
cafe attributes it to a weaknefs in the
Periftaltick motion of the Inteftine.
The following obfervation will fhew
how the part was affected in a fimilar
inftance.

A boy about twelve years old was
brought the twenty-ninth of January
1756 to Stevens's hofpital. Six years
before he began to grow coftive, not
difcharging by ftool for feveral days,
his Belly enlarging by degrees: This
habit fo far increafed, that he ftooled
but once in three weeks, and then
nearly emptied the whole Inteftine at
an effort, but it was full fix weeks fince
he difcharged when he came to the
Hofpital; his Belly was exceeding pro-
minent, and to fight it appeared like a
tympany,

tympany, attended with a fhortnefs of Breath, and total lofs of appetite, great thirft, and a partial fuppreffion of urine. In three weeks from his arrival at the hofpital, without emptying the Inteftine, he died.

On opening the Body the next day, we found the whole cavity of the Belly almoft filled with the Colon; its mean diameter was about four inches, and filled uniformly throughout with foft contents, except at the fphincter of the Rectum, where the contents were fomewhat indurated. The fmall Inteftines were crowded into the leaft fpace they could poffibly be contained in, including nothing but vapour; the Liver, Spleen, and Stomach, were with the Diaphragm forced up into the Cheft, compreffing the Heart and Lungs; the Kidnies were found, and the right Ureter of a due fize; but the Ureter on the left Side, dilated to five times its natural diameter, was, with the pelvis of the Kidney proportionably dilated, filled with urine.

As

As in an habitual Ischuria then, proceeding from the Bladder, this receptacle may lose that power of restitution to express the urine, and even suffer dilatation thereby, so may the Colon likewise lose that power, which co-operating with the Muscles of the Belly and Diaphragm, force out the residuum of the aliment, after the finer is absorbed by the Lacteals; and by this so great may be the collection as to press the circumambient parts and incommode their functions, so far as they depend on the free motion and due size of these parts, and even force them into the Cavity of the Chest, lessen its Cavity, check inspiration and the motion of the Heart, and even stop it at length. And this enlargement of the Belly may be distinguished from that arising from extravasated water by its want of fluctuation, compared with the gradual suppression of the Fæces.

We may likewise note too, that the pression of the Colon in given circumstances is greater on the left than the right Ureter; for the Colon being extended beyond the bounds of nature is no objection, forasmuch as the distension was proportionable throughout the Intestine, and yet the right Ureter was not extended by its pressure; so that the infarction tended to make the difference of pressure visible. We may likewise note too how useful are warm gentle eccoprotics, where there is reason from the costiveness of children to suspect weak Bowels; to which may be added, sweating the Belly to conserve its contents from enlarging: And further, that the tumid appearance of the Bellies of infants may be sometimes caused by fulness of the

In-

Inteſtine, as at other times, by the enlargement of the Liver, Spleen, and Meſentery.

And we may likewiſe gather in ſome meaſure the reaſon why clyſters are generally of ſignal uſe in ſuppreſſions of urine, and of the plentiful efflux of urine ſucceeding; for all infarctions of the Inteſtine being removed by clyſters, the Ureters are more at freedom to vibrate, and conſequently the better expreſs the urine coming down from the Kidnies: And the tumefaction of the Kidnies from the Blood and Urine confined therein being thus removed, the pain in the Back, the conſequence of their tume-faction, ceaſes.

Coſtive habits are ſometimes ſaid to be the effect of ſtrong Bowels, foraſmuch as the bibulous orifices of the Lacteals draw off the humid contents, and leave the reſt ſo exſiccated that the Inteſtine is ſcarce able to expreſs it; but ſtrong Bowels ſignify themſelves by the dryneſs and hardneſs of their con-tents; whereas weak Bowels in coſtive habits ſignify themſelves by the ſoftneſs and quantity of their con-tents and intumeſcence of the Belly; and thus ſtrong Bowels are ſo termed from the intenſity of the ab-ſorbing powers of the Lacteals; and weak Bowels from the weakneſs of the powers of the Lacteals, and want of periſtaltick motion in their Fibres.

We may laſtly note too, that as reaſon denomi-nates parts weak from their ſoftneſs and impotence in moving, as in the Muſcles, and from their being liable to fluxions, as the Brain and Lungs, and from their being given to Congeſtions, as the Liver in
ſome

some diseases of the Viscus, so we collect from this observation that Parts are constituted weak in the human system sometimes not from reason but dissection.

OBSERVATION V.

Flat Worms.

In spring 1752, a woman about forty in Stevens's complained of a constant inquietude, and chiefly in the night, a want of sleep, a fulness of the Belly, a costiveness, and a want of appetite.

She passed per sedem an immense length of white flat worms, half an inch long, and linked together.

At the same time another about fifty had a fulness of the Belly, and a rumbling of the Intestines, who passed a vast quantity of like worms by siege.

Another about thirty, who had a fulness of the Belly, and an enormous appetite, vomited up an innumerable multitude of the same worms.

In summer the same year in Stevens's, a boy who had convulsive tremors

mors and great faintnefs at times, ftooled an endlefs length of the fame.

In the fame year a young man of twenty, who had voided per fedem thefe worms for ten years, had a conftant gnawing pain in the left Hypochondrium.

By thefe examples then an inquietude, a fenfe of fulnefs, a coftivenefs, a want of appetite, rumblings of the Inteftines, convulfive twitches, tremors, and pain in the Hypochondrium, may be fymptoms of flat worms in the Inteftines, and an enormous appetite and vomiting may indicate their exiftence in the Stomach.

* From the motions and irritations of the Inteftines arife the inquietude and rumblings; which irritations being propagated to the origin of the Nerves, from the fenfible and irritable Fibres of the Inteftines, and reflected thence to the Fibres of the Mufcles, may produce the convulfive twitches and tremors; the fenfe of fullnefs and want of appetite from their number, and the pain in the Hypochondrium to their gnawing and fixing themfelves to the Inteftine, for the head of this worm when viewed in a microfcope exhibits two circles of fangs, as we fee in the cut given us by † Tyfon, who defcribed this worm with very great exactnefs; and the enor-

* Galen de Caufis Symptomatum, C. 3.   † Tranf. Phil. v. 3. 131.

mous

mous appetite may be owing to their abforbing the Chyle by the multitude of mouths in the fides of their divifions defcribed by the fame author, and the vomiting to the fame fort of irritations which occafion the rumbling and other motions by confent with the inteftinal.

And thefe obfervations teach us that thefe worms are incident to either fex, or to any age.

Whether this worm is one only, or a chain of diftinct worms adhering to each other as fwarms of bees do, or whether it be the fame in fpecie with that whofe head and tail are defcribed by Daniel Le Clerc *, whoever defires to be further informed of, may confult the different opinions and controverfies compiled by this learned author, who being more follicitous about the mode of formation and ftructure than figns of their exiftence, I have endeavoured to fupply the deficiency out of the foregoing obfervations; which collection of fymptoms however cannot be held as decifive of their exiftence in the Inteftines, without the antecedent or concomitant appearance of fome.

OBSERVATION VI.

Round Worms.

In June 1752 a boy of fifteen in Stevens's had a conftant flux of faliva

* De Lumbricis Genevæ 1715, 4to. Cap. 8, C. 9.

from

from his Mouth, a rumbling of the Belly, a devouring appetite, a loosenefs and senfe of motion tending from the bottom of the Belly towards the Diaphragm.

In the fame month he paffed by fiege three worms, round, red, and four inches in length, and of the thicknefs of a goofe quill.

OBSERVATION VII.

In December 1752 a boy of feven years old died of a worm fever. I found in the fmall Inteftines fifty-fix round worms, whofe mean length was fix inches, of the diameter of a goofe quill in their middle, defcending fmaller toward their terminations and white in colour; they filled the fmall Inteftines completely, and were immerfed in mucus; Nothing was in the Stomach or great Inteftines but mucus and vapour. He died the Day before, and was not emaciate.

The fymptoms of round worms therefore may fometimes be a flux of the falivary glands, a rumbling of the Belly, a devouring appetite, a loosenefs and fenfe of motion tending from the bottom of the Belly toward the Diaphragm; and it appears that round worms, by multiplying, enlarging, **devouring the aliment**, and feeding the Blood with the impurities of their fæces, may raife a fever and terminate in death.

Round worms, from their greater activity and ftrength, may raife ftronger vibrations in the Inteftines than flat ones, which being propagated to the falivary glands, may draw them by confent into preternatural fecretions, and fo difturb the Inteftines as to produce a loofenefs, and that motion of the **air** which always exifts in the Inteftines, **to keep** them from collapfing, fenfible by the rumblings; the devouring appetite being caufed partly by their abforbing the Chyle, and partly to that uneafinefs the perfon feels when the Inteftines are empty, exciting a defire of food to fatiate, and prevent their fucking and preying on the Membranes of the Inteftine, and the tending of fomething from the bottom of the Belly to their endeavouring to get at the aliment above them.

The ftructure of the Mouth, Stomach, Inteftine, and other interior organs of this worm, we have from Tyfon, with a caution not to give the powder of the worms as fpecifick, left more be regenerated from it.

SECT.

S E C T. VI.

Of the KIDNIES and BLADDER.

OBSERVATION I.

*Total Suppreſſion of Urine from weak-
neſs in the Bladder.*

A Young woman, whoſe name was
Bolton, having ſuppreſſions of
Urine after lying-in, came to St.
George's in London in the year 1753.
The Catamenia were according to nature, and ſo were the inteſtinal excretions both in quantity and time; the
moſt approved medicines for theſe in-
dications could not bring away the
urine, and others were exhibited without effect. A bliſter between the ſhoul-
ders once cauſed it to flow ; but when
the power of the Flies was abated it

I 3   ſtopped

ſtopped as before, ſo that for half a
year it was drawn off with the catheter
twice a-day, and ſo ſhe continued till I
left the hoſpital in 1754.

Now as the catamenia were according to nature
in time and quantity, and the birth not attended
with diſtreſſing circumſtances; the ſuppreſſion could
hardly be attributed to the Uterus, which by preſſing, as being charged with catamenia *, or other-
wiſe ſwelled, might ſtop the egreſs of the urine;
and the ſame may be argued of any preſſure it
might ſuſtain from the Rectum; nor was it owing
to a ſtone or caruncle in the Bladder or Urethra,
for the catheter and even the Finger had an eaſy ingreſs, without perception of impediment in the introduction: Beſide, ſhe never had been troubled
with nephritick ſymptoms which are uſed to antecede the ſtone in the Bladder; and from the continuance of the ſuppreſſion it could not be deduced
from an hyſterick or ſpaſmodic affection of the
Bladder, Ureter, or Kidnies, foraſmuch as ſuch diſ-
orders are not of duration; and from the eaſy ingreſs
of the catheter and Finger, it could ſcarce be effected by a tumor of itſelf; it was therefore cauſed by
a weakneſs of the Membranes, or loſs of elaſticity,
which Membranes in a ſtate of health co-operate
with the Muſcles of the Belly to expreſs the urine
dimitted from the Kidnies. Now as this weakneſs
commenced in the time of gravidation, it muſt have

* Ca'en de Locis affectis, lib. 6. 5.

been

been caufed by the preffure of the ulcers, which by
retaining the urine, ftrained the Membranes till they
were unable to contract.

We may alfo note by the way, that fome medicines are elective in their actions. Were the actions
of cantharides by mere ftimulus indifferent to all the
Membranes, why fhould it be exerted on the urinary parts the rather than on the Membranes of the
Inteftinal Canal, which are much more fufceptible
of impreffions from irritating caufes than the Membranes of the Kidnies, Ureters, and Bladder are?

OBSERVATION II.

Total Suppreffion from Weaknefs in the Bladder.

A man about fifty, the 24th of July
1756, was feized with a total fupref-
fion of urine, which was drawn off
the fame day, as alfo the following
day, with the affiftance of the catheter, but he made water after without affiftance till the 26th of November, when the fuppreffion returning,
he was brought to Stevens's in a high
fever, with very great pain; the whole
Hypogafter was tenfe and elevated, and
he had a ftrong inclination to vomit.
The urine let forth with the catheter,

I 4 the

the elevation fubfided, and the tenfion
and fever remitted : The urine drawn
off was of a dark colour and muddy,
about three pints in quantity. For a
month after the urine was let out in
like manner twice a day, morning and
evening ; the left Tefticle fwelled and
abfceded, painful fenfation was propagated in the direction of the Spermatick Chord to the Back ; and a fungus
fhot out of the abfceding Tefticle. In
fome time after a whitifh mucus came
off in the urine like the mucus of the
nofe, when the fluxion of the nofe is
duly concocted, but fubfiding in the
urine, and unattended with pain in
the region of the Bladder.

The fymptoms therefore of the Bladder being full
of the urine, in a fuppreffion at the Bladder, are an
intumefcence of the Hypogaftrick Region, attended
with a fever, and inclination to vomit, and pain
through the Belly.

The fame fort of fuppreffion in the preceding was
unattended with the pain or fever, the Membranes
of the other fex being more diftenfible and moift,
and confequently propagating in their time of tenfion lefs painful fenfations, and fcarce effecting inflammation

flammation like the tenfe and rigid Membranes of the male.

Was the inflammation of the Tefticle and fubfequent abfcefs owing to the frequent introduction of the catheter? For an inflammation of the Urethra will fometimes arife from this caufe, and the fpafms of the Fibres of the Vas Deferens refulting poffibly therefrom, being propagated to the Tefticle, might draw its Veins or the whole Tefticle into fpafms and inflame it? Or was it owing to the ftricture of the Tendons of the Mufcles of the Belly fqueezing the Chord? For you will obferve pains and ftricture of the fpermatic Chords and Tefticles in affections of the Nervous Membranes of the Lower Belly, to which thofe Mufcles are given to confent; and it has been likewife obferved by **Areteus** * in affections of the Colon and other Inteftines.

Moreover while I was confidering the fungus of the Tefticle, it occurred to me that it bore fome analogy to the fungus fhooting from the Brain in fome wounds of the Head; and that poffibly it might be fome fort of argument of the Brain being of the glandular kind.

OBSERVATION III.

Total Retention from a Stone in the Bulb of the Urethra.

A man about fifty, who had been mowing down hay in fummer 1752,

* De Caufis & Signis diuturnorum morb. c. 8.

was

was feized with a total fuppreffion of
urine, and prefently bled, and plentifully purged, but without effect. That
evening he was brought to Stevens's in
miferable torment, where he raved immediately, and fevered, and fo died.

On opening the Lower Belly next
day we found the Bladder rent at its
fundus, and the Pelvis filled with the
urine, caufed by a black ftone, of the
fize of a filbert, in the bulb of the Urethra, which ftopped it compleatly.

From this calamitous incident then we may fee the
dangerous effects of a total fuppreffion of urine on
the male, from a ftone in the Urethra, if the removal of the ftone be deferred: Had he been carried directly to the Houfe, and the incifion inftituted in the Perinæum, which is eafily and readily
done, he would have been undoubtedly faved.

We may likewife in fome degree eftimate the
ftrength with which the urine is expreffed from the
Kidnies and Ureters, or the intenfity of the efforts
of the Bladder to free itfelf from the urine, or the
ftrength of both thefe caufes acting in fucceffion;
for how active the Kidnies are in forcing the urine,
we may collect from their effects on the Ureters
when they have been repeatedly plugged with ftones
near their terminations in the Membranes of the
Bladder,

Bladder, or when the Ureters are preſſed by any cauſe; for they will be often ſo enlarged by ſuch cauſes obſtructing or preſſing the Ureters as to emulate even the Inteſtines themſelves *; the column of urine dimitted from the Kidnies, and ſtill expreſſed, by increment, expanding their Membranes.

And that equally fatal effects may follow from too long retention of urine, which by gradual increment dilates, and at length inflames in this ſex, we are aſſured by Fabricius Hildanus †, who tells us, the famous Tycho Brahe, the Daniſh aſtronomer, by ſtaying too long at an entertainment in Prague, had his Bladder overcharged with Urine, and thereby inflamed, by which he fevered and died. And Dominicus Panarola ‡ ſays, that he found in three ſubjects who died of this diſeaſe the Bladder exceedingly diſtended by the multitude of Urine, which in ſome amounted even to twenty pints, which ſhews thoſe Bladders had loſt their powers of reſtitution; for the healthful Bladder reſtores itſelf in the egreſs of the Urine to the leaſt ſpace it can poſſibly contract; and he alſo obſerves this diſorder is unheeded at firſt, but in proceſs of time It diſtempers the Bladder, and conſumes them. Nor indeed is the reaſon difficult to ſeek; for the Bladder having loſt its elaſticity, like an inanimate Bladder juſt taken from a ſubject, collapſes into itſelf, and thus continues till the ſucceeding Urine enlarged it to its firſt dimenſions, when from the loſs of its

---

* Panaro'a, Pent. 4. Cbſ. 31. Hanoviæ 1643.   † De tuend. Valetud. Franc. 1682.   ‡ Pen.. 1. Obſ. 27.

spring the Urine stagnates, till let out with the instrument; and at length the Bladder, by being repeatedly strained, and its Tunics squeezed between the incondensible Urine within, and the power of its connection at the bottom of the Pelvis at every the greatest distension, for want of due circulation in its Tunics (in which too very probably the Blood extravasates) it gangrenes or ulcers, corresponding in proportion to the Intestines in an hernia; for inflammations of the Intestines are given to terminate by gangrene rather than apostem, when they do not resolve, or it suddenly gangrenes, as it probably might in the case of the illustrious Brahe.

And as the Bladder fills and dilates either from inattention of the mind, as in deep meditation or sleep; or from necessity, as in assemblies, entertainments, or riding, even to a loss of restitution, so likewise has it been observed to fill and enlarge by reason of want of due communication with the medullary tracts in the Spine * or Head; so that the irritation of the Urine, or the straining of the Fibres, do not signify themselves by the propagation of painful sensation. Now this state of the Bladder cannot be distinguished by any other means than the causes which antecede paralyses, nor even by all of these, unless they are visible, as in great shocks or wounds in the spinal Marrow, or compression thereof by luxations of the Vertebræ: For if a paralysis of the Bladder is caused by extravasations of water or Blood, or congestions in the Membranes about

* Peverovicius de affect. Renum & Veficæ, c. 2. 40. Leidæ 1636.

the

the medullary tracts where its Nerves have their origins, it will be difficult if not impoffible to affign
the precife caufe, unlefs fome exterior Mufcles are
affected with coldnefs, numbnefs, and impotence, as
they are in paralyfes from thefe caufes; and there
diftinctions are of fignal ufe for the mode of cure in
a refolution of the Bladder by compreffion near the
origins of its Nerves, fuch as bleeding, purging,
and fparing diet would be totally ufelefs where the
Membranes are ftrained by the preffure of the Uterus, and the quantity of Urine being kept in thereby, or in the other caufes of inattention, or neceffity
of fituation as above; for thefe affections of the
Bladder are treated by cold bathing, blifters, or cantharides inwardly given, and great temperance in
drinking, efpecially at night; for if the quantity be
fuch as being fecerned copioufly, paffes down to the
Bladder, it will contribute to conferve the inlarge-
ment of the Bladder, and if the quantity be great
will really do fo * from the inattention of the mind
during fleep to the motions of the parts, and the
irritations of their contents.

Laftly, we may note too, that violent exercife
will move a ftone out of the Bladder into the Urethra, and caufe a total fuppreffion of Urine, as it
will out of the Liver or Hepatic Duct, or out of the
Gall Bladder and Cyftick Duct into the common
Duct, and caufe a total fuppreffion of Bile.

In the preceding we have feen a total retention
arife from weaknefs of the Bladder, and from the
authority of Beverovicius that the fame may arife

* Galen de Locis affectis, lib. 6, 4.

from a Paralyſis of the Membranes ; and we have
ſeen too the Urine ſuppreſſed by a ſtone in the bulb
of the Urethra.   But Fernelius tells us *, the Kidnies, as other vaſcular parts, are liable to inflammation, though but rarely from their firmer texture,
and deſcribes their ſymptoms and conſequential effects.   Having myſelf had an opportunity of ſeeing
ſuch inflammation, it may not be improper here to
recite it, together with its antecedent cauſe and ſymptoms, ſuch as I have obſerved them.

OBSERVATION IV.

Total Retention from an Inflammation
in the Kidnies.

A man about thirty, in March 1755,
by drinking muddy porter to an exceſs,
had his Urine totally ſuppreſſed, with
great pain in his Loins, Hypochonders,
and Belly, attended with a high fever.
The ſuppreſſion continued five days,
and was at length removed by the repeated exhibition of clyſters, bleeding,
and purging, with infuſions of ſenna,
manna, and ſalts ; but the pains in the
Hypochonders remaining were at laſt

---

* De Part. Morb. & Symp. cap. 12.

removed

removed by the ufe of an electuary made of rhubarb, foap, and fyrup of althea.

Note, there was no intumefcence of the Belly in this cafe, nor pain in the region of the Pelvis.

A total retention therefore may arife from fwelling and inflammation of the Kidnies, when fuch is the difpofition of the Blood, that the Urine cannot be drawn off by the Kidnies, and this caufe of fuppreffion is diftinguifhed by the heavier pains in the Loins and Hypochonders compared with the antecedent errors committed ; for if the Inteftines agree in fpafms with the Kidnies, the confent and fympathy ought to be ftronger between the Colon and Kidnies, feeing the Colon is more immediately connected with the Kidnies, which is not the cafe between the fmall Inteftines and them ; and if the Kidnies draw no Serum from the Blood, either becaufe in the mafs flowing to the Kidnies the Cruor bears too great a proportion to the Serum, or becaufe the Serum is of fuch mode of parts that it will not pafs to the uriniferous Tubules, the Kidnies fwell and comprefs the excretory Ducts, and thus totally cohibit all fecretion ; fo when the Cortex of the Brain fwells, and the medullary tracts are clofed thereby, the propagation of the mandates of the will is ftopped ; and when the medullary tracts of the Retina in an internal opthalmia are preffed by the fwelling of the Retina, the perception of the
appulfe

appulfe of the Vertex of the rays, and the power of
receiving ideas of colours is prevented. Thus then
is the fyftem loaded with hot fcalding fluid, which
moving in the nervous Membranes, excites fenfations of pain, and in the irritable Membranes, vibrations attended with the fymptoms and ferment of
a fever, even exclufive of the inflammation, and yet
more in conjunction with it.

If this total retention arofe from a fault in the
Bladder, it would have fignified itfelf by the fymptoms in the fecond obfervation; fuch are an intumefcence in the Hypogafter and the reft. And if
it arofe from gritty infarctions, it would probably
have been preceded with fymptoms, and fucceeded
with emiffion of gravel, which it was not: It was
therefore owing to the Kidnies themfelves, not infarcted with ftone or fand, but infpiffated Cruor
and Serum.

OBSERVATION V.

Strangury from fcalding Urine.

Reynolds was about fixty years old,
when by drinking ale and brandy at a
burial, as the fafhion among the common people of this ifland is, in the beginning of December 1760 he complained of a ftrangury, attended with a
violent pain through the whole Hypogafter,

gafter, which painful fenfe was propagated along the Spermatick Chords and Tefticles; and fucceeded in a few days with a copious fediment of a thick mucus in the Urine, white and vifcid as bird-lime. Emollient clyfters and laxative infufions were exhibited with fome decrement of fymptoms to the end of the month: The 29th the Urine was bloody, and he was fomewhat eafier. In the beginning of January I gave him tincture of cantharides, fome drops in the day out of mint water, with an intention to ftimulate the Bladder to an expreffion of the mucus, which kept the Urine from paffing off as faft as it came to the Bladder; but by this means he made bloody Urine with great pain; there was nothing fo ufeful to him as large draughts of boiled milk and water taken cold, or a weak infufion of althea mixed with the milk. In the beginning of February he feemed to recover, the Urine ftill depofiting the fame mucus, and fo it continued till June 1761, when the pain

K   and

and ftrangury had a total ceffation, but left fomewhat of an impotence in retention of Urine.

Now from his being free from fuch fymptoms before this excefs, and their immediate fucceeding, we may fay, that the Serum of the Blood, overheated and acrid, when feparated into the Bladder, did fcald its Membrane, and caufed it to excern that abundance of mucus, which, fubfiding in the Urine toward the orifice of the Bladder, fuppreffed the free exit of the Urine, and thereby encreafed the pain, micturition, and by fympathy the tenfion of the Belly, and in confequence of that tenfion the pains of the Chords and Tefticles, as we feemed to infer in the fecond obfervation ; for he was tried in the beginning of his ailment with the catheter, but it could not gain admittance, being inhibited by the multitude of mucus.

So then we may fafely affirm, that an acrid Urine may ftimulate the Bladder to an excretion of more mucus than it ufed to do, to lubricate and defend the Membrane from the falts of the Urine, when the Blood was cool and in a ftate of health, juft as the Inteftines are given to do in an habitual dyfentery, or the Trachea in a fluxion on the Membrane of the pipe ; and this irritation may be attended with Blood in the Urine, as it is in a dyfentery by abrafion of the natural defence of the interior Tunic ; fo the Blood may come from the Bladder only as it does from the Kidnies, fometimes either by their weaknefs, dilatation of their Arteries, and uriniferous

ferous Tubules by rarified Blood, erofion by ulcers,
or the friction of the ftones ; and this fecretion of
mucus may not a caufe total fuppreffion of Urine,
but that fort of fuppreffion attended with drops and
pain ; and that this is the cafe, will appear yet more
from the following

OBSERVATION VI.

Strangury from fcalding Urine.

A man about fixty came to Stevens's
in fpring 1756, his Urine came off by
drops with very little intermiffion,
and a conftant acute fenfe of fcalding ;
the Prepuce inflaming adhered over the
Gland, and the Urine collected between the Gland and it; the Skin being flit, the Urine was difcharged : but
the heat, pain, and micturition ftill
continued, which pain was feverely felt
in the Bladder. He was fent to Swad-
ling Bar waters, and drank the water to
ten pints in a morning for fix weeks,
and was thereby cured. This man
was fearched in the beginning, but no
Urine flowed out, nor was there any
ftone perceptible to the catheter.

Now

Now as there was no ftone perceptible to the ca-
ther, nor any Urine flowed from the introduction,
we may juftly affign the caufe of this painful micturition to the heat and erofive difpofition of the
Urine, which fretted the Bladder, and drew it into
painful fpafms, fo that whenever the leaft drop of
Urine came, it was neceffitated to exprefs it, or
the fame might arife from a feparation of a fcalding
Rheum in the Tunics of the Bladder itfelf. Now
the Swadling-Bar water, by cooling the Blood and
Serum in the whole fyftem, and weakening and di-
luting the fharpnefs of its parts, and in confequence
the Urine derived therefrom, and wafhing off the
acrid particles from the Tunics of the Bladder, and
by perfevering therein, totally removed all this difpofition.

And becaufe any fpecifick power this water may
be endued with, in diftempers of the Bladder, is not
generally agreed to, it is probable that milk and
water boiled together, and drank to the fame quantity cold daily, would have the fame effect; for
the water dilutes, and the milk heals, and both
drank cold run off by the ureters almoft as foon
as taken into the Veffels.

From this and the preceding it looks as if this affection was rather incident to people in years.

O B-

O B S E R V A T I O N VII.

Stone in the Bladder.

In March 1753 a man about thirty-
five, of a lean habit, came to St.
George's hofpital in London: for three
years he had a conftant pain in his back,
loins, and obtufe pain in the region
of the Bladder. His Urine in the night
dripped away involuntarily, and in
ftraining to ftool he felt the hard contents of the Rectum ftop, requiring a
very ftrong effort to force it over the
obftacle: He was fearched the 16th,
and we heard the Stone hit againft the
ftaff; after due preparation he was
cut, and a Stone extracted. Its figure
was fpheroidal, fomewhat depreffed,
without angles or afperities, and weighed four ounces two drachms Troy, and
was very compact. The Urine flowed
through the wound for fome weeks,
and as it gradually healed it returned
in proportion to the Urethra, and

K 3

about

about the end of April he went out recovered.

The preparation was a clyster the evening before the operation, so that by the emptiness of the Intestines the efforts after operation might be longer suspended, and thereby the wounded parts be free, as well from the pressure of the Muscles of the Belly forcing the Intestines toward the Bladder, as from the pressure of the contents of the Rectum in their passage through the Gut. After operation a solution of Gum Arabick was drank copiously to abate the sharpness of the Urine, and the whole Belly fomented with flannels expressed from revolving infusions to prevent and discuss internal inflammations.

The involutary dripping of the Urine was caused partly by the gentle irritation kept up in the Membranes of the Bladder from the Stone, and partly for that the orifice of the Bladder was held somewhat open in an horizontal position of the Trunk when laid in bed: The obstruction to the egress of the contents of the Rectum being owing to the pressure of the stone against the Rectum ; and probably the pain in the Back and Loins to the Kidnies being partly
infarcted

infarcted in the ftone and fand, which in paffing
along the Ureters excited thofe tearing fenfations in
the Loins before and during the formation of the
Stone in the Bladder.

OBSERVATION VIII.

Stone in the Bladder.

In May **1753** was brought to St.
George's in London, a man who from
his infancy had been ufed to make
bloody water on any extraordinary motion and exercife. He had a pain in
his Back, and fudden ftoppages of water when he ftood erect; he was fearched on the 21ft, and a ftone perceived.
On the 25th he was cut, but the Stone
in extracting, being foft and very large,
crumbled in the forceps, and was taken
out by pieces; yet toward the end of
September the wound healed, and he
went to the country.

All the pieces taken out in this operation were of the colour of free-ftone,
and fimilar in texture.

The

The bloody Urine very probably came fuch from the Kidnies, as from their friable compages, and their abounding with Blood, being more liable to Bleedings from the friction of ftone or gravel, than the Ureters or Membranes of the Bladder; the ftoppages of Urine, when erect, arifing from a change in the pofition of the Stone, which in the act of emiction was preffed on the Neck of the Bladder.

OBSERVATION IX.

Stone in the Bladder.

In October 1753 a man about thirty was taken in at St. George's, who for fome years had made bloody Urine, with a pain in his Back, and voided fand, with frequent fuppreffions of Urine. He was fearched three years before at St. Thomas's in Southwark upon thefe fymptoms, but nothing extraneous was perceived in the Bladder; when he was fearched at St. George's fomething was felt obftructing the inftrument, but we could hear nothing hit againft the catheter as is ufual in fearching. He was cut however on the 26th, and feven foft brown Stones,

each

each of the fize of a chefnut, and like it in figure, were extracted ; they were hard in the center, but toward their furface confifted like clay juft wrought for burning to bricks.

It appears then that there may be more than one Stone exiftent in the Bladder, and yet the perception to the Catheter next to none, or but very obfcure : but as thefe were fymptoms indicating the exiftence of Stone in the Bladder, though the Catheter could not make it quite evident, yet in conjunction with the fymptoms an obfcure perception is fometimes fufficient to juftify the attempts for extraction ; and this may be one ufe of comparing fymptoms with their caufes, and recording the effect.

And we further obferve, that it is the foftnefs of texture in the Stone which fometimes caufes the obfcurity : For if thefe Stones were encyfted in the Tunics of the Bladder *, the orifices of the Cyfts, as being narrower there than any other fection of the Cyft, muft be opened for their egrefs.

OBSERVATION X.

Stone in the Bladder.

In December 1753 a man of feventy years old, in exceeding great mi-

* Sharp's critical Review, fect. 2. Lond. 1750.

fery from a Stone in the Bladder, was received at St. George's; thus he had been for fome weeks without any intermiffion of pain, fleeping fcarce three hours in twenty-four, and that too interrupted with pain.

The Perineum and all the ambient parts were livid, and when the catheter was introduced, purulent matter flowed out of the Bladder along the fides of the inftrument. Thefe circumftances did by no means favour the operation, yet as he defired it extremely, it was thought proper to hazard his recovery, as he muft have died of the pain, inflammation, and fever, if left as he was; the Stone extracted was very hard, granulated, and rough in its furface, of the fize of a pullet's egg. He had perfect eafe from the time of operation, but died in a few days after.

A Stone in the Bladder therefore, and efpecially with afperities, may by its irritation and friction inflame the Bladder, and caufe it to fuppurate; an ufeful caution to thofe who have Stones in their Bladders, to be careful in the mode and continuance of their exercife; for if a rough Stone, even with-
out

out the addition of agitation of the body, but merely
by the repeated closing of the Bladder on the Stone
in its systole at the end of every emiction, can produce such an effect, how much more likely would
it bring on the same collection of symptoms, assisted
with the repeated friction of the Stone and **Bladder,**
in walking, or constant succussion in riding?

And we may also observe, there are cases where the
operation must be instituted, though the symptoms
be all unfavourable; in order to relieve the person
from the extremity of pain, and especially as the
consequence of the operation is a matter of incerti-
tude; for no man can say, but that if you remove an
irritating cause, the pain and inflammation ceasing by
a removal of that cause, the dead and suppurated
parts may dissolve and fall away, and others rege-
nerate in their places, even in advanced years. Almost similar to which is the case of the English
Consul at Padua *, who was so teazed with a Stone
in his Kidney, that by intreaty he prevailed with
Dominicus Marchetti to try an operation before held
impracticable, and cutting through the Loins and
Kidney he extracted two or three Stones; but the
wound growing fistulous by the Urine filtred through
it, another afterwards offered itself, which being
taken out he was totally free from pain for the future. But this indeed was rare good fortune, for
had the Stone been complicated with the Kidney, or
branched throughout it like coral †, as they sometimes are, even though the operation had succeeded
as far as the Kidney, the event were desperate.

* Transf. Phil. vol. 3. 188.   † Idem, vol. 7. 532.

O B-

OBSERVATION XI.

Stone in the Bladder.

In October 1753 a very fat man, about fifty, was cut for the Stone in St. George's hospital, and one of the size of a small pullet's egg was extracted, very hard and compact; his complaints were recent not above three weeks before, and after a tedious fit of the gout. His Pulse intermitted some days after operation, and he had returns of profound tremors, but they wore off by degrees, and the wound healing he went out recovered.

Now as so large a Stone can hardly be conceived to form in three weeks, it appears there may be a Stone of some size in the Bladder without indication by the symptoms. Nor indeed is it repugnant to more general experience; for Lossius*, an eminent physician of Devonshire, tells us, that Sir William Pool, who died of old age in that country, had a Stone in his Bladder fourteen ounces in weight, with an hole in its middle, through which the Urine flowed, without ever being conscious of its exist-

---

* Obs. 53. Lond. 16; 2.

ence

ence or growth. And yet more extraordinary is the
the fpiculated Stone, fent by the Marquis de Cha-
mont * to Sir Hans Sloane, which notwithftanding
the active life the perfon who had it in his Bladder
conftantly led, yet had no perception of its exiftence, till the total fuppreffion which brought him to
his death in a little time after. The reafon of which
very probably is, thefe Stones adhere fo as not to
roll to the neck of the Bladder, and are covered
with the mucus of the Bladder, fo as to excite no
irritation, until at length by violent exercife or
fome turn of the body they are forced from their
hold, and fo fignify themfelves, by fuppreffion of
the Urine, pain, and micturition.

OBSERVATION XII.

In May 1754 another very fat man
was cut for the Stone in St. George's,
who was fomewhat turned of forty;
and a very hard Stone, of the fize of a
hen's egg, extracted; he had returns
of profound tremors as the preceding.
His Pulfe funk in a few days after, and
his Mouth and Tongue grew dry, and
thefe fymptoms increafed, and in a
week from the operation he died.

* Tranf. Phil. 9. 172.

Fat

Fat bodies then are liable to the accretion of the Stone as lean bodies are; that is, the difposition of the Blood, whereby it is predominant with oily parts, is no impediment to thefe petrifactions from forming in the urinary parts.

OBSERVATION XIII.

In November 1753 a man about forty was brought to St. George's, he had a pain in his Back, fuppreffions of Urine, and pricking pains propagated down his left Thigh and Leg, even to his Ancle. Being fearched, the Stone was heard to hit againft the ftaff. He was cut, and a very great Stone extracted with the utmoft difficulty; the Stone was very compact, and hard as marble; its figure was fpheroidal, fomewhat depreffed, and weighed eight ounces and a quarter Troy. In fome weeks the wound healed up, and he went out tolerably well as to the confequences of the operation, but the pricking pains down his Thigh and

Leg,

Leg, with frequent retentions of Urine, continued.

Now the Stone being removed, and the fuppreffions of the Urine, and pains in the Thigh, and downward perfifting, it appears thefe symptoms are not of neceffity connected with the exiftence of a Stone in the Bladder, but are fometimes symptoms of Stone or gravel in the Kidney or Ureter, to which caufe only they could be affigned in this place. And as Stones may grow to fuch a fize in the Bladder, and as the danger of extraction is in proportion to the fize, it were to be wifhed thofe who are confcious of the exiftence of a ftone in the Bladder, would apply in time for an operation, whofe hazard increafes by delay; and that the operation be inftituted as foon as ever it is known in children, feeing the Nucleus will foon draw the fand coming down with the Urine to its own increafe. A very large Stone Dr. Hunter ufed to fhew us at his lectures taken from the Bladder of the perfon who died of it, of fo enormous a fize, that it muft almoft have filled the Bladder in its mean dimenfion; and another is kept in the library of Trinity College at Cambridge, taken after death from the fame fex, whofe weight is upwards of thirty-three ounces, the hiftory and defcription of which Dr. Heberden has given us *.

* Tranf. Ph'l. vol. 11. 1005.

The

The fize of the Stone in our obfervation may be gathered from the following fection ; A the greateſt plane, and the other B at right angles to the for-mer, which I meaſured at the time.

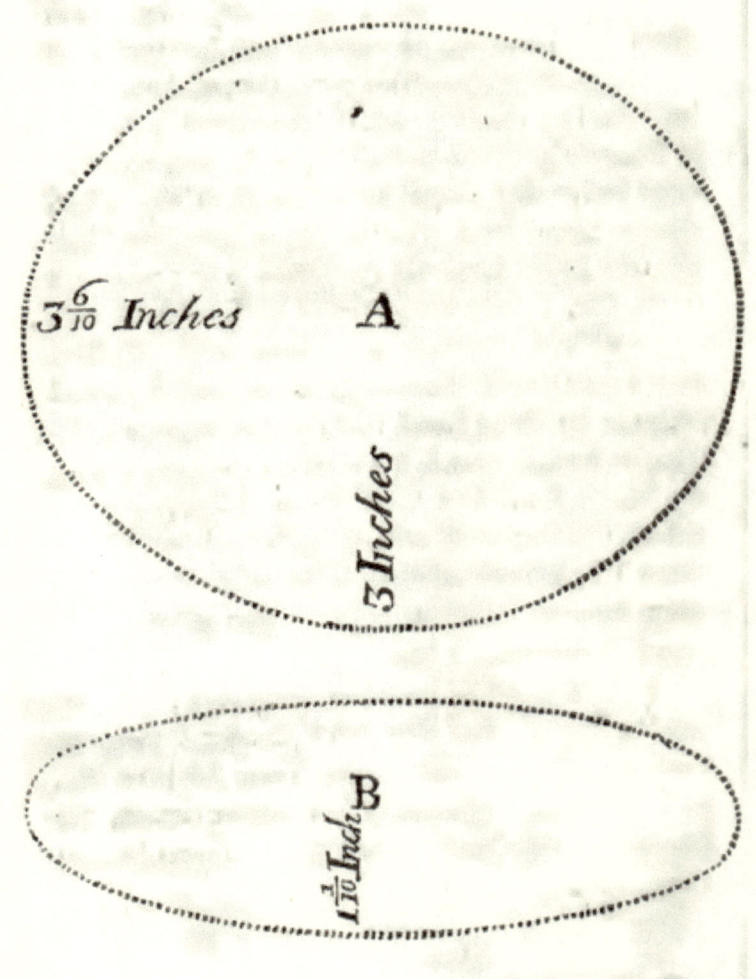

OBSER-

OBSERVATION XIV.

Stones in the Kidnies.

In 1753 there was a boy in St. George's Hofpital about fourteen, who had been cut for the Stone two years before, yet after operation, when the wound was healed, he had fupprefiions of Urine in all pofitions of the Trunk with refpect to the Horizon, and pains in his Loins, and chiefly the left, and was fomewhat incurvated that way; his countenance fweaty, pale, and tumid, and exhaled an urinous vapour, and fell at laft into a dropfy afcites.

Now comparing this with the preceding obfervation, fuppreffions of Urine from obftructions in the Kidnies, or infarctions of the Ureters, may differ from thofe arifing from Stone in the Bladder, by their being unaltered in changes of the pofition of the Trunk with refpect to the horizon; the moifture of the fkin likewife, with the urinous vapour it exhaled, feemed to indicate a want of due feparation in the Kidnies, and may fometimes ftrengthen our con-

L   jectures

jectures of the exiftence of Stone in the Kidnies, when taken in conjunction with other fymptoms.

Moreover, we may infer that an afcites is a poffible confequence of a want of fecretion in the Kidnies.

OBSERVATION XV.

Stones in the Kidnies and Bladder.

The firft of November 1753, a tall red haired man, about forty, was brought to St. George's in London to be cut for the Stone, who had pains in his Loins, and made bloody Urine, with frequent Micturition and fuppreffions of Urine for many years : He came from the country at a great diftance, and fuffered exceedingly by the agitation of the waggon in which he was carried, infomuch that he fevered and died before he was fearched or otherwife meddled with.

The next day, on opening the body, and taking out the Kidnies, Ureters, and Bladder, and dividing the Kidnies through their greateft fections,

there

there was found in the Pelvis of the left
Kidney, a triangular hard ftone of the
fize of a chefnut, and like it in colour:
The right Kidney was diminifhed in
fize, and its lower part a heap of Hy-
datides, and its upper part interfperfed
internally with red fand: The Ureters
were diftended to treble their natural
diameters; and in the Bladder was a
very compact round ftone of the fize
of a hen's egg, and fix ounces in
weight.

It fhould feem then as if Stones were formed firft
in the Kidnies, and defcending to the Bladder, concreted there to form this large Stone; for that fome
Stones defcended appeared from the enlargement of
the Ureters, which by reafon of the ftopping of
Stones near their termination in the Tunics of the
Bladder, were extended with the columns of Urine
exprefled by the Kidnies: And as there was but
one Stone in the Bladder, fo we may conjecture that
it was formed by an union of thofe which defcended,
and we may alfo conceive this union is perfected by
means of animal gluten fecerned in the Tunics of the
Bladder; for if an animal gluten is found among
joiners to unite vegetable Fibres fo firmly that even
the natural power which holds together thefe Fibres
is not fuperior, and like as we fee the mucus in the

Sto-

Stomachs of black cattle unite together firmly the hairs thofe creatures fwallow, into a ball, conftituting our indigenous Bezoar; fo poffibly it may be the nature of the mucus fecerned in the Bladder, by the irritation of the defcended Stones, to draw them together, and unite with them into one uniform body, where cohefion and texture may equal even the hardeft in degree; which mafs, at every Syftole of the Bladder, will be condenfed, and its formation into hard Stone perfected thereby.

We may likewife here as in obfervation the third, remark, and by experience too, the ftrength of the action of the Kidnies, which in every fucceffive Syftole forcing their Urine are able thereby to expand fo ftrong a complication of Membranes as the Ureters are compofed of.

And while I was confidering the exiftence of the ftone in the left kidney, and the want of it in the right, though there had been evidently Stones in the right, by the expanfion of its Ureter, Pifo's affirmation occurred to me, that of an hundred bodies afflicted with the Stone in the Kidney, upwards of eighty had it in the left * : now feeing the authority of Pifo is of great weight, his difcoveries in the nature of difeafes being highly commended by the fkilful †, it may not be foreign to the prefent bufinefs to endeavour to find the moft probable reafons, taking the affirmation for granted, at leaft fo far, that of Nephriticks the majority are there affected.

---

* De Morb. è ferofa colluvie 283, Paris, 1633.   † Liber aureus, Webfer de apoplexia 226, 1675, Scaphufi.

First

First then, if the Colon has lacteals, as the other Intestines have ‡, reason tells us that its contents ought to be more exsiccated by how much nearer they accede to the Rectum, and therefore will the Ureter be the more compressed on the left than the right side; but the Colon crosses the Ureter where it coincides with the Rectum, and where the Membrane (Mesocolon) is narrower than at any other part of the Colon, and where the Ilium bone resists the pressure on the side of the Ureter opposite to that whereon the Intestine rests; therefore will the Ureter be more constricted upon this account, than where the Colon crosses the right Ureter; for there the resistance on the opposite side of the Ureter arises from the soft parts; and therefore will the Urine at every infarction of the Intestine be more retarded in the left than in the right Ureter, and consequently more in the pelvis of the left Kidney than in the right; and where the Blood is predominant with hard parts, will be more disposed to deposit these in the left Kidney than in the right; and truly I saw myself in a boy about twelve years old, dissected at Stevens's in the year 1756, who died of an infarction universal and proportionable through the Colon, the left Ureter three times the size of the right, and, together with the Pelvis of the Kidney, filled with the Urine, which Pelvis was enlarged into a Sacculus of a considerable size; nor was the right Ureter expanded in like manner: Now if we add moreover the situation of the emulgent vein on the Aorta, by which

‡ Winslow, Sect. 8. 219.

L 3

the

the Blood of the vein may be conceived to be retarded by the beating of the Aorta, and in confequence the Veins of the Kidney to fuffer fome degree of Intumefcence, and the urinous tubules fuch degree of preffure whereby the Serum moves not fo free and uniform as where there is no fuch preffure, and from the want of that uniformity and freedom of motion the fandy parts are thereby the more given to ftop and adhere to the fides of the Tubules and run to each other, than in the right Kidney, we fhall have a much more rational account of the appearance than what Dodoneus and Pifo have left us.

OBSERVATION XVI.

In May 1754, a boy of ten years old was cut in St. George's Hofpital, and two ftones taken from the Bladder, one of the fize of a walnut, and the other lefs, which had a concave depreffion correfponding to the convex furface of its companion, both of which furfaces were exceeding fmooth.

It fhould feem then from the form and polifh of thefe ftones, the Bladder has a motion independent of its Syftole in expreffing, and Diaftole in receiving the Urine; for if Blood moves through its Tunics as it does, and fecretion is performed therein,

it

it is evident the whole Tunics throughout muſt have an eaſy ſucceſſion of vibration propagated in them, independent of the Syſtole in every emiction ; or if the Bladder be only capable of Syſtole and reciprocal Diaſtole, this motion conſpiring with the motion, of the whole ſyſtem in eaſy conſtant exerciſe, and the motion of the urine in its ſucceſſive influxes from the ureters and effluxes from the Bladder, did effect it ; for if there be more than one Stone looſe in the Bladder, the Urine in the influx will move them eaſily againſt each other ; ſo will it alſo in its efflux.

OBSERVATION XVII.

Stone in the Bladder.

On the thirteenth of April **1753**, in St. George's Hoſpital, a child of four years old was cut for the Stone, and one extracted of the ſize and form of a walnut. In a few weeks the wound healed up and he went out well.

From this obſervation then we eſtimate the time in which a Stone of a given ſize may form in the Bladder ; for at the utmoſt it could not be above four years and a few months concreting, ſuppoſing that it began to form before the time of nativity, as

Dominicus Panavola * and myfelf have obferved of the jaundice.

And comparing thefe with all the foregoing, it appears that any age from four to feventy is liable to the Stone.

By thefe examples then it appears, that a pain in the Back of fome continuance, an involuntary dripping of the Urine in bed, a ftoppage of the contents of the Rectum in ftraining to ftool, an obtufe pain-in the region of the Bladder, fudden ftoppages of Urine when erect, may be held as fymptoms of the Stone in the Bladder; and thefe fymptoms are ftronger to indicate its exiftence, if bloody Urine, and voiding fand, and pricking pains down the Loins and inferior extremities, were antecedent; for there are fymptoms of Stone in the Kidney by the thirteenth, fourteenth, and fifteenth obfervations, which are antecedent to Stone in the Bladder by the fifteenth.

And all this rightly underftood, confidered, and difpatched, it feems probable to me, the accretion of the ftone is often independent of errors in the antecedents of difeafes, forafmuch as children are as liable to the Stone as thofe of advanced years : thofe of inferior conditions, as well as the great and rich ; fat as well as lean bodies, where the errors committed are either none or very diffimilar.

It feems therefore, as if that peculiar difpofition, which is productive of fuch parts as line the Blood and uriniferous veffels of the Kidnies, Ureters,

* Pent. Ob. vide etiam Tranf. Phil. vol. 2. 1063.

or

or Bladder, were native with us; though I do not deny the possibility of its being adventitious; for if hard particles of bodies can pass the Lacteals, as they do by the experiments of Lyster * and Musgrave, so any other hard particles of sizes and shapes like to the former, may likewise pass into the Blood, and floating in the emulgents, stop there, and give origin or nucleus for a larger concretion.

But whether adventitious or native, let us see what anatomists have found touching its origin in the Kidnies, that, led by the senses, we may yet nearer accede to the truth, and with more assurance deduce the real mode of formation.

The first then (as I know) who has given us an account of what he saw in dissection, is the late Dr. Mead †: He tells us, that he dissected a boy of five years old, who died of nephritick complaints, attended with a vomiting and loosenes, in whose Kidnies and Ureters the calculous matter had here and there put on various forms of concretion; the first foundation was an aqueous limpid humour, which lactescing by degrees, shot into crystals, and they uniting, hardened into stone: And Haller ‡ in his 34th observation says, he found the Bellinian ducts filled with an orange-coloured mucilaginous matter in a boy and in a man, but in a woman whom he dissected in October 1741, it was white and hard, and rattled when he shook it, so that it would have soon concreted into perfect stone; now by compounding these observations, we may say from dif-

* Transf. Phil. vol 5, 255-6.   † De Imp. Solis et Lunæ, p. 56, 1756.   ‡ P. 84, 1755, Lusannæ.

section,

section, that the Stone has sometimes its origin from a saline lymph first growing turbid and shooting into chrystals, which harden into Stone : now seeing it is the nature of the saline liquors under circumstance of rest or languid motion, and when saturate with salt, to run into crystals of shapes such as the salt is in spe ie, we need not appeal to a spirit in the Kidnies, Gorgon-like coverting the Serum into Stone ; moreover we may at other times conclude it owes its origin to a mucilage or lentor, which stopping in the Kidnies, hardens into Stone, and probably at times to both these causes acting in conjunction.

But in order to know how the Blood or Serum is predominant with hard parts, I evaporated a gallon of my own Urine to dryness, and found at the bottom of the glass vessel two drachms weight of red grit. Now if my Urine is saturate uniformly with sand in this proportion, there must pass off with the Urine from day to day forty-five grains of sand, and in a month three ounces nearly, provided my Urine from day to day, at a medium, is three pints. Now if a hundredth part of the sand subside and rest in the Kidnies, then will there be in a month thirteen grains nearly, and in a year two drachms and one half nearly, for concreting into Stone ; and in ten years eight ounces. Now putting some of this sand last April in every pellucid circle of Culpepper's Microscope, I viewed it first with N°. 1, and the particles appeared largest but less distinct, and in every successive glass smaller, but more distinct, and the appearance was as of a multitude of red particles of not very different sizes, surrounded

with

with very pellucid fparkling bright particles, as of falt or fparks of diamonds, which pellucid particles I likewife faw throughout the whole furface of a ftone, taken from a perfon lately by Mr. Croker, which ftone weighed fix ounces and a drachm troy.

Again on the 26th of July I evaporated with a lamp-furnace five ounces meafure of the Urine of a gentleman's coachman, who conftantly voided fmall Stones, from the fize of a hemp feed to that of a cubeb feed, or a fmall white pea, and who had alfo a fmall Stone in his Bladder; and was taking a few drops of the common foapboilers lie every day for fome weeks, and found in the bottom of the china bowl fixty grains of a whitifh chalk and grit : Now if this man's Urine was faturate uniformly through-out twenty-four hours, in three pints of Urine there muft have paffed off nine ounces of earth, which probably was owing to the great activity of the lie. Now thefe experiments prove the Urine has a great portion of firm particles, fwimming therein, and in confequence that the Blood from which thefe Urines were derived, has therein a great portion of like parts, as the diffections of Mead and Haller fhew they ftop fometimes in the Kidnies, and there con-crete ; and thefe concretions may the more readily form, if they find a diverticulum by reafon of any flight ulceration exiftent in the Kidney, to reft in.

And thus we have found the materials of the Stone by diffection, experiment, and reafon, toge-ther with the mode of formation in the Kidney, de-rived from a native or acquired idiofyncrafy at firft.

Now

Now the particles with this foundation soon enlarge, and going on, increasing in succession of time, and different places in the Kidney, may possibly at length equal the Kidney itself in size; that is, fill the whole membrane, by abrading the intermediate Parenchyma, as we see in the petrified Kidney kept in the curiosity-room in the college.

But sometimes the accretion commencing in different parts of the Kidney forms several Stones. of any size or shape, which continuing there by their attrition, as being moved against each other by the constant vibration of the Kidney, abrade the Parenchyma of the Viscus, and leave nothing but a bag full of stones, which has been long since observed by Fernelius * of Amiens, one of the most learned and ingenious physicians of his time.

But if the fabulous Infarction or the abrasion of Stones prevail universally in both Kidnies, a renal Cachexy, attended with a drowsiness, shortness of breath, pain and weakness in the back, vomitings, and fluxes of the Belly follows, which terminates the scene; and yet life may be preserved even to longevity with one or more stones in each Kidney, and of some size, provided they trespass not too much on the Kidney; nay with one Kidney only, so that the other continue free to drain off the Urine, or even without both, if what some authors affirm be just, that where the Kidneys were both wanting the Intestines grew parenchymatous and fleshy, and by such mode of organization drained off the super-

* De part. morb et symp. cap. 12.

fluity

fluity of Urine in form of a loofenefs from time to time. So that we need not be aftonifhed at what Bellin * afferts, that when a Gland is wanting to fecern a fpecies of humour, that nature may conftitute a Gland for the purpofe. Such fhifts in the animal fyftem are fometimes contrived.

Should Stones form in the Kidney, and arrive at a given fize, without being incyfted in the Vifcus, or without the veffels in their Interftices, then may they be hurried off with the Urine, and down the Ureter into the Bladder, where uniting, they may form one or more Stones as they happen feveraily to receive increment by the fubfidence of fand out of the Urine, or unite among themfelves, and collectively receive the like fubfidence; for if there be no nucleus, fuch as a fmall Stone or other permanent body to receive or attract, the fand will float in the Urine and pafs therewith, or it fubfides on the Tunic, and wafhes off with the fucceeding Urines; for the mucus of the Tunic, for want of that compreffion it receives from the capillary veffels in the Kidney at every fyftole of the Vifcus, will hold it at fome diftance from the Tunic, fo the Urine getting behind it loofens it from the Tunic and carries it away.

But if the fand of the Urine fubfide on the Nucleus, it will be attracted by the Nucleus, which having no internal motion or vibration as the Fibres of the Tunic have, may be the more inclined to preferve the fubfident particles; and when the Urine flows out of the Bladder it will, by fuffering com-

* De Miffione Sanguinis, p. 100. Francfort. 1698

preffion

preffion from the Bladder, be yet more condenfed
on the furface of the Nucleus, and the particles forced
to a ftate of ftrict cohefion; for the attraction of particles not fpherical and contiguous, and without agglu-
tinizing medicines, is from the doctrine of powers exceedingly increafed by the leffening the diftance, even
with a power greater than their gravity *; but Stones
formed by the fubfidence of fand on a Nucleus,
fhould have, when cut through, a lamellated appearance, as ftones formed by feveral fmall ones
defcended from the Kidnies a granulated one, both
of which are to be found in the collections of the
curious.

Now the caufes of the Stone, as of other difeafes,
are either immediate or antecedent; and the immediate are either native with us, as when the Stone
is caufed by ill conformation of the Kidney, or by a
difproportion of the particles compofing the Blood
(*materiæ immoderatione,* in the language of Galen and
Fernelius) in its original fabrick, at the time it was
fet a going by the heat of incubation; or thefe immediate indifpofitions arife from the antecedents of
air, diet, exercife, fecretions, fleep, and paffions of
the mind.

That the air, by its fenfible qualities of heat, cold,
drynefs, or moifture, can induce this diforder, unlefs by affecting the cuticular difcharges, and even
then, is difficult to conceive: but if the particles of
true permanent air arifing from the folid bodies of
the earth pafs into the Blood with the food, as they
undoubtedly do, and are forced to a diftance lefs
than any given one in their paffages through the

---

* Newton's Princip. Sect. 13. prop. 85, 86.

Membranes, they may from the nature of the particles of this fluid unite into hard particles, and be the flamen of a Stone; for bodies conftituted with repulfive powers, as the particles of air are, when they come into contact, run to each other, and unite with the ftrongeft powers of attraction, which is clearly deduced from the doctrine of powers: and it is known the animal calculous and vegetable concretes correfponding to it in proportion, yield a confiderable portion of air by folution, and forcing their particles afunder in diftillation.

And if the light thin volatile air, or a Blood-globule as fome think, can give original foundation, yet more furely will the quantity of drink we take in the day, whether it be the lighteft water, or a preparation of it, as in beer, or drawn from vegetable juices, as wine or fpirits. The waters in all parts of the earth, either ftanding, as in ponds, or running, as in rivers, or falling out of the air, as rain, or derived from fprings, are more or lefs faturate with hard parts; more in fome countries and places than others; more in the waters of the Sein or Rio Blancho, than in others; which hard parts may, by getting through the Lacteals, as they do by the experiments of Mufgrave and Lefter, ftop in the Kidnies and form there : And the fame may be argued of the tinctures of animal and vegetable Fibres we are eternally feeding on.

Now if the Blood, replete with thefe parts, is not duly digefted and broken by the vibrations of the parts through which it moves, and which vibrations are weak and feeble in fedentary or other inactive

life,

life, it is evident it will, as all the humours flowing with a languid motion through the excretory
Ducts of Kidnies, or other fecerning Glands, be yet
more inclined to let go their particles on the fides of
thefe Ducts ; for in the veffels of Blood themfelves,
where one would lefs expect it from the velocity of
its motion, have Stones been found, unlefs we are
exceedingly deceived by authors.

And as to the times of fleep, this affection of the
whole man as it is in found fleep, may come under
the above article of a fedentary life and flow fecretions, and its effects made out by fimilitude of
reafon.

Laftly, it is fcarce to be imagined that any affection of the mind, as of grief, joy, fear, anger, and
others, however they agitate the fyftem of nervous
parts and membranes, can give origin or increment
to the Stone in the Kidney, unlefs it be by the unequal motions raifed in thofe glands, and even then
it is difficult to conceive it ; and yet I have known
a fit of the Stone in the Kidney from fudden fear.
Now taking the exiftence of one or more Stones in
the Kidnies for granted, let us look to their confequential effects.

Firft then, the increafe of fize of one Stone, and
the attrition of feveral by the Kidnies, Syftole, and
reciprocal Diaftole, we have already fpoken of.

Now as Stones have been known of fome fize
exiftent in the Kidnies, without the perfon being
ever confcious of their exiftence, we cannot be abfo-
lutely certain when the fandy or faline Lentors begin
to infarct and diffufe themfelves through the Kidnies ;

nies; the reafon of which is, the Kidnies are of fuch obtufe fenfations, they do not tranfmit with painful ideas their diftreffes, as more fenfible parts do; their nerves and thofe of other Glands probably ferving little other purpofe than their fecerning motions, and motions of vital unition; whereas the Skin and Inteftines, Trachea, Ureters, and Bladder, being more expofed to injurious caufes acting immediately with very little, or without alteration, have their Nerves as well or rather more conftituted for fenfibility than other parts at a diftance from and out of the reach of fuch deftructive actions: and indeed the commencement is fometimes fo recent in life, if not coæval, as we faw in the feventeenth inftance, that the perfon is unable to fignify it, even though he were confcious by tranfmiffion of painful fenfation.

But having obferved myfelf a pain in the back, fucceeded with acute pains in the Ureters and Bladder, and voiding of fand, and cord-like fpafms of the colon, where there was no very great reafon to fufpect a confirmed Stone in the Kidney (for the perfon could ride forty miles a day on a hard trotting horfe without bloody Urine) it feemed to me as if the Kidnies, being nearly infarcted at the terminations of the Arteries and beginning of the Veins and urinous Tubules with fandy Lentors, did fwell and excite the pain in the Back, and by their redoubled vibrations and impetus of the fucceeding columns of Blood in every artery, thefe fandy Lentors were forced off into the Pelvis of the Kidnies, Ureters, and Bladder, along whofe fides thofe fharp pointed fpiculæ moving and adhering here and there,

M did,

did, by fretting the tender and irritable Membranes
of the Ureters and Bladder, excite the tearng acute
fenfations felt after the pain in the Back had fubfided,
and all in the direction and region of thefe parts;
yet this prefumes an almoft total infarction to make
it fenfible: But if the Kidnies are but partly conftipated, fo that the Blood of the emulgent **can pafs**
round the obftruction, and let its ferum fall into the
Pelvis of the Kidney, then may **the** infarcted **part**
give origin **and gradual** increment **to the Stone,**
without fenfation **of** pain, and the confcioufnefs of
the formation; fo then the only way by which we
can judge of this difpofition incipient, is by the paffing of fome of the fand down the Ureter, which
being fenfible of it, will fignify its exiftence, as
will the Bladder in conjunction; **and this** is the
mode of effecting what are termed fits of the gravel,
at leaft to me it feems to be fo.

Now if the Kidney **has** feveral ftones therein,
fome of which being near the Pelvis, and lefs than
the Ureter in Diaftole, and polite in their furface,
they may find their way to the Bladder with toler-
able eafe, **as a walnut fwallowed will through the**
Inteftine; whether they have changed fituation for
the better is juft as it happens, but fometimes being
larger than the Ureter in Diaftole, or more environed
with afperities, **they** draw the Ureter into fpafms,
and ftop their own defcent; this is indeed a very
nice and critical **cafe,** and calls for inftant attention; for by the fpafms and vibrations it raifes in
the Inteftines, which may **be** propagated through
all the nervous Membranes, and by the unequal
commotions

commotions through the whole fyftem, it even threatens life itfelf, and is termed a fit of the Stone in the Kidnies. But another effect of a larger ftone than can pafs down the Ureter is the making bloody Urine; and this arifes fometimes by the meer motion of the Kidney, and its friction againft the Stone, and at other times by fome extraordinary motion of the Body as in riding or other modes of travelling ; nor is the making of bloody Urine fo dangerous an incident of itfelf, but it fignifies a difpofition creating ulcers ; moreover the extravafated Blood may partly diffufe itfelf round the Stone, and by there corrupting deftroy the Vifcus.

C U R E.'

As fits of the Gravel in themfelves are painful and troublefome, and fignify the future formation of ftone, we ought to begin our proceedings immediately, left they run into union, as we faid before.

In order then to prevent thefe effects, we may begin by wafhing off the mucilage, falt, and fand from the Kidnies, by drinking large draughts of honey and water boiled together, and fet afide till cold, repeatedly in the day, or chalybeate waters, or conftant, riding which is better than all ; for by increafing the Blood's motion in the Kidnies, all congeftions in the convolutions of the Arteries are cohibited, and which alfo by encreafing the fecretion of Urine will have the fame effects in the Bellinian Ducts; and this is done, not by changing the texture of the Blood, or by irritation, as all diuretics

M 2   do,

do, but by raifing the vibratory motion of all the
organical parts in the whole fyftem, and which will
thereby promote and preferve the due conftitution
in all parts ; but if either by reafon of fome other
indifpofition of the Body, or the avocations of bufi-
-nefs, the cure by riding cannot be complied with, then
befide the foregoing, the foap pills taken to an
ounce or lefs, as it agrees with the Inteftines, together with the oyfter-fhell lime-water, now in univerfal ufe, is requifite, as the foap by its oil lubri-
cates the urinous Tubules, and by its lixivial parts
diffolves and ftimulates, as the water does alfo by
the experiments of Dr. White ; and this courfe is
not to be continued for a month or fo, but years,
nay, during life itfelf ; for I have lately feen one,
not exceeding twenty-two years old, who having
been cut for the Stone twice in London, and at
each time had one taken out, has lately had one cut
from the Scrotum at Stevens's, another yet remaining behind ; fo predominant is the Blood, either by
native or acquired idiofynecrafy, with firm parts in
the bodies of fome, and difpofed to form concretions
in the uriniferous parts.

But fhould one or more Stones form in the Kidney, without our being confcious of their formation,
until arriving at a given fize they fignify their exiftence by an obtufe pain in the region of the affected part, or bloody Urine, or extraordinary exercife ; then are we are to look partly to its folution,
and to prevent its increafe, and be cautious againft
what is termed the fit of the Stone in the Kidney or
Ureter ; for people have lived to advanced years
                                                with

with Stones in their Kidnies, unattended with much inconvenience.

With refpect to the folution of the Stone in the Kidnies, it is true the Stone was very hard and compact in the feventh, tenth, thirteenth, and fifteenth cafes ; in the eighth ; foft and brittle in the ninth, foft, without being gritty, and did therefore probably differ in fpecies and effence ; forafmuch as it is rational to conclude, that bodies differing in degrees of cohefion, and in the fecondary qualities of colour (for the hardeft were almoft black, the foft and gritty was grey, and the foft without being gritty of the colour of fnuff) differ alfo in fpecie and effence ; an ungrateful reflection indeed to one who wifhing mankind well is himfelf nephritic : But yet at the fame time it ought not to difcourage us from trying the menftruums which are known to diffolve fome Stones therein immerfed out of the Body ; for it may be poffible fo to fate the Blood and Urine with thofe medicines, that they fhall be a menftruum for the lefs compact Stones, and becaufe it is impoffible for any one to prove the Stone in the Kidney is indubitably of the harder kind. But here in our endeavours to folve the Stone, or prevent its increafe, we are to look to the abrafion of the Kidney, or the creating or increafing ulcers in the Vifcus, which diuretics indifcriminately ufed, and perpetually, may be given to do, by reafon the Urine faturate with the foap and lie, for inftance, becomes exceeding detergent ; but the Stone whofe folution we are endeavouring to accomplifh ought rather to exift in the Pelvis of the Kidney, where all the me-

dicinal

dicinal Urine dripping from the Mammillary Proceſſes waſhes its ſurface.

But in order to prevent its increaſe, the diſpoſition in the Blood is (if poſſible) to be removed, as we ſaid in fits of the Gravel ; and this rather by ſome ſolutive medicines and changes in diet, than diuretics and riding : But we are to obſerve, the Stone may exiſt, as we ſaid, in the Pelvis of the Kidney, and thus it comes under the foregoing article of ſolution ; for if the medicinal Urine ſolves it, it is evident the Stone exiſtent in the Pelvis, however it may be diminiſhed, cannot increaſe: But if the Stone is at a diſtance from the Pelvis, and is encyſted, or exiſt in the Interſtices of the Veſſels without communication with the Blood and Urine, which is poſſible, neither can it increaſe further, nor yet be diminiſhed. But if the urinous Ducts terminate in the cyſt, and the Urine have an eaſy exit therefrom, then will the Stone be waſhed, and may either admit of ſolution, or its increaſe be cohibited by the diſpoſition of the Urine to depoſite its fæces there, being removed by the medicines giving to the Blood and Urine lubricity, and ſome degree of ſtimulus, ſuch are the ſoap pills taken to a drachm or two daily, ſo as not to force too ſtrong a diureſis.

Another effect of the exiſtence of a Stone in the Kidney, is the abraſion of the Veſſels, and making bloody Urine, and the hazard of producing ulcers and apoſtems in the Kidney, which are more deſtructive than the Stone itſelf, which as we ſaid will be the conſequence if the extravaſated Blood reſt in the Sinus containing the Stone. Now this calamitous nitous effect may possibly be prevented by abstaining from excesses in feeding, which load the vessels, and from excessive drinking, especially claret and punch, and other heating and stimulating wines and spirits, and riding on horseback or other violent exercise, by which the system is too much agitated. I have observed that a bottle of red wine or shrub punch drank over night, has the day following so raked the Ureters that the patients have scarce been able to go about their ordinary business, but have lolloped on a couch the whole day. Dr. Sydenham in in his own case (a large Stone in the Kidney) found great relief by purging with manna, dissolved in whey, once in a week, from the pain in his back (which I knew to be just myself) and made less bloody Urine, and bore easy motion in a coach tolerably well. And indeed this practice is very agreeable to reason in many respects ; for by removing the contents of the Colon, the Kidnies and Ureters are more at freedom to vibrate and expand, to secern and let go their Urine, than when pressed by the contents of the Colon, and the vibrations of the Kidnies more easy, and the frictions between the Kidney and Stone lighter and less frequent, by reason all organical parts, when their contents are obstructed from moving, redouble their efforts to free themselves. Again, by the purging, the whole system of Vessels is drained of its load of Serum, which by reason of the weakness of the Kidnies, as partly infarcted, are unable for the due discharge of their office ; which Serum, when the Vessels are turgid therewith, is apt to exsude from the internal Membranes, and cause

M 4   such

ſuch ſymptoms as are natural to theſe parts; that is
to ſay, vertigoes, epileptick fits *, numbneſs of the
Muſcles, paralyſes, and even apoplectick ſymptoms, if from the Membranes of the Brain; humo-
ral aſthmas and a dropſy of the Cheſt, if from the
Membranes of the Cheſt; and ſometimes too a
dropſy of the Belly, if its exſudation is from the
Membranes of the Lower Belly; or at leaſt raiſe
painful ſenſe of eroſion in all the ſenſible Membranes, unleſs the ſuperfluity exhale in form of an
urinous vapour copiouſly, as Carolus Piſo * obſerved; or in form of an urinous looſeneſs, which has
been obſerved by the late Dr. Hoadly †; or at leaſt
the internal Membranes and Fibres of the Muſcles
will be ſo humid, that they perform their buſineſs
but feebly. Dr. Sydenham has likewiſe directed a
large draught of ſmall beer going to bed to dilute
the hot acrid humours, and waſh from the Kidnies
any new fabulous matter congeſtive in ſleep. This
practice of Sydenham I know to be juſt, but with
due limitation. The reſpect I have for the memory
of this great and experienced phyſician is ſuch, that
I tried every precept of his with a ſtrange prepoſ-
ſeſſion of his ſkill; for ſure he underſtood things
wonderfully: I ſay with limitation; for if you over-
do this buſineſs, you will find next morning your
head loaded and unapt for thinking, and ſometimes
too a pain in your Back, and almoſt total inability
to go about even the moſt eaſy actions.

* De Morb. e ſeroſa Colluvie.   † Lectures on Reſpi-
ration, p. 97.

The

The Kidnies, as all organical parts, are ever in a state of eafy vibration, provided they are not influenced by morbid caufes. Now it is evident if there be one or more Stones in the Kidney, as being extraneous bodies, they will difturb the uniformity of the fecerning and vibrating motions; and thus may Stones raife fuch motions by their irritation, that the Kidney fhall fhift them from their former place; and if they are near the Pelvis, one may poffibly drop into the head of the Ureter, or may fo turn the Stone in the Kidney or its Pelvis as to draw on the fit; in which, as we faid, not only the Kidney, Ureter, and Bladder, but the whole volume of the Inteftine and Stomach, is drawn into the acuteft fpafms, threatening even life itfelf; and indeed I once faw a gangrene of the Colon from a lefs active caufe than this, that is, from fpafms occafioned by a Stone's mutation of place in the Gall Bladder. If the fit arife from irritation of Stone, or from motion raifed in the Kidney by external caufes, the cure is the fame.

But in order to prevent this dangerous incident, we muft abftain from violent exercife, as riding, bowling, leaping, or over-walking, and any other motion by which the fyftem is too much fhaken or contorted, and from ftrong diuretics, exceffive drinking, fudden paffions of the mind, and preferve the Colon free of a load of contents; for thereby it will not prefs on, heat, or difturb the Kidney itfelf, or too much prefs the Ureters, which by returning the Urine toward the Kidney would alfo difturb it, feeing motion is raifed in all the organical parts by

stopping

stopping the progreſſion of the fluids therein contained.

If, notwithſtanding our care, a ſtone gets into the Ureter, and draws on ſuddenly the ſymptoms attending the fit, and the perſon be full of Blood and young, bleeding is requiſite by all means to prevent the effect of too much Blood thrown unequally through the parts by the ſpaſms, which may be attended even with extravaſation itſelf, and then are we to try what an infuſion of ſenna and manna given by ſpoonfuls, and often repeated, will do ; for if it ſtays on the Stomach and paſs into the Inteſtine, it may poſſibly force off the contents of the whole canal : but if this is impracticable at the time, by reaſon of the vomiting and tenſeneſs of the Belly, then will it be proper to endeavour at the ſame effect by clyſters not over ſtimulating, but rather emollient with ſome irritation ; for by this means all preſſure of the contents of the Inteſtines being removed, the Ureter will be at more freedom to expand on any remiſſion of the Spaſm : Then are we to try what emollient infuſions, ſuch as that of althea, not in too great a quantity, the warm bath, oil of almonds, taken by ſpoonfuls, in order that theſe decoctions and oil, getting with the Urine into the Ureter, or with the Blood, through its Membranes, may lubricate and relax the Membranes of the Ureter, and with greater facility let the Stone deſcend. Beſides all this, it will be requiſite to aſſiſt with a good doſe of laudanum ; for Archibald Pitcairn * tells us, the

* Element. Med. C. 12, 25, Lond. 1718.

famous

famous Dr. Hervey, by taking a large dose of liquid laudanum in the fit, discharged more than one Stone during the doze it occasioned ; and as it is the nature of opiates to suspend the motion and stricture of Fibres, whether subservient to the will or not, the effect no doubt was owing to the relaxation of the Membranes about them : Of what use vomiting in the fit can be I really cannot conceive ; for if the Stone is impacted in the Ureter, it is clear the force of the Muscles of the Belly will scarce remove it, its motion being rather the effect of the easy Diastole of the Ureter, and consequent Systole ; and this repeatedly and succeffively corresponding to the succeffive easy relaxation and compreffions of the intestines on their contents ; and such are nearly the ways taken in the fit by Piso Beverovicius, and Sydenham, who were all very learned and experienced physicians, and themselves nephritick ; and I have myself been an experienced witnefs of their wholesome effects ; and univerfally in sandy Lentors of the Kidnies, Ureters, or Stones in either of them, I would have the great Inteftines kept free of contents, forafmuch as every the leaft fand or Stone falling into the Ureters, draws them into ftrong fpafms, and the Colon by confent, and this almoft perpetually ; which I have known at times fo ftrong in the Colon, that it refembled the fenfe of a cord tied ftrictly about the Hypochonders ; and by this means it is the Inteftines are lefs difpofed to let go their contents than in thofe who are free from fuch complaints ; and fo in a fecondary manner by keeping the

2   preffure

preſſure of the Colon ſtronger on the Ureters, does
the Stone contribute to its own formation.

Thirſt is an almoſt perpetual concomitant with
this diſorder, and principally in the morning. At
time of riſing therefore it may be of uſe to drink a
diſh or two of weak chocolate, if it agree with the
powers of the Stomach ; the chocolate quenches the
thirſt, raiſes the oppreſſed motion of the ſyſtem by
its warmth, and yields ſome degree of internal lubricity to the Fibres of the veſſels, through which
the urinous Lymph or the Urine itſelf flows, and
ſheaths them from being fretted with the ſaline or
terreſtrious ſpiculæ ; if it is heavy on the Stomach,
a diſh or two of tea at breakfaſt with the family will
aſſiſt to dilute it.

Any light food of beef, mutton, fowl, fiſh, broths
of all kinds, exempting thoſe of firmer texture,
ſuch are ſpiced and baked meats, or pickled, may be
taken at dinner, with ſoft white wine and water ; tea
in the evening, and at night a draught of the ſmall
ſoft ale that the brewers in the county of Wicklow
make ; for it is a ſort of drink that agrees with ne-
phritics much more than any of the malt kind, even
the fineſt London porter, which carries with it more
irritation. The county of Wicklow ale is clear and
ſoft, and moderately ſpirituous, and heats but little :
it raiſes the motion of eaſy micturition * without diſ-
turbance : A draught of this going to bed has brought
on a good ſound ſleep, a comfort nephriticks do not
often enjoy ; and indeed it is agreeable to reaſon

---

* Fits of eaſy rarefaction and eaſy condenſation. Gliſſon
de Rachitide, C. 12.

that strong liquors going to rest should prevent sleep, chief nourisher in life's feast, as the Poet says, and composer of human cares and pain; for if the secretion of Urine is not so full as nature requires it should, the vessels of the system will be charged with too saline a Lymph, which by irritation keeps the body in a state of slow febrile effervescence, which is attended with restlessness, a want of sound sleep, and great thirst in the morning.

When a Stone has got out of the Ureter into the Bladder, its exit should be promoted, lest it serve as a nucleus for a larger, or unite with others into a larger Stone.

Now this may be attempted either by diuretick waters, whose feruginreous parts stimulate the Kidnies to secern; and if the Stone be not too great, it may be carried out with the tide of Urine; for the danger of forcing the Stone from the Bladder is by no means equal to the danger of forcing the Kidnies; for should the Stone be stopped in the Urethra, it can be readily removed by incision, which ought to be immediately instituted, lest possibly so fatal an event might happen, as in observation the third; besides diureticks too, there are medicines which force the Bladder itself without increasing the quantity of Urine; among which the most effective that I know, is the common soap boilers lie, or the lie of the London Dispensary; a few drops of this out of any simple water twice or thrice in a day, increased or lessened according to the effect: The Urine on taking the lie presently grows muddy, and the Stones are soon put into motion; but in the exhibition great

cir-

circumfpection is to be ufed, left the Kidnies contain a large Stone, the motion of which might precipitate the perfon into inftant hazard of his life; which is alfo to be confidered in the ufe of chalybeate waters or other diureticks. Chefelden * gave one one day with another forty drops, for thirty-one days, and the perfon voided innumerable fmall bits of ftone; which effect I have feen of it nearly correfponding to the account he gives; but in the returns of pain caufed by this medicine, inftead of purfuing it without intermiffion, we muft abftain, drink decoctions of althea, and gum arabick, and oil of almonds, that the Urine by its foftnefs and lubricity, and fome degree of tenacity, may alfo contribute.

But if a larger Stone exift in the Bladder than can be removed by lubricity and ftimulus, and it be attended with no great or immediate inconvenience, as frequent returns of fuppreffion of Urine or acute pain, and the perfon be advanced into years, I had rather commend fuch a management of diet and exercife as may prevent the dangers of the tenth and fifteenth obfervations, that is, a cooling diet, moderate in quantity, temperance in drinking, efpecially heating and ftimulating liquors; and eafy motions, as in a coach with fprings; for the danger of a fmooth Stone not liable to inflame the Bladder, is not fo great as the danger of operation, feeing that wounds and lacerations of the Bladder in the operation are given to end by gangrene in thofe of advanced years on account of the hardnefs of the Fi-

---

* Tranf. Phil. vol. xi. 992.

bres, and their want of good Blood to effect their unition.

But if the Stone is rough, and by its irritation threatens inflammation, and keeps up pain, and caufes fuppreffions of Urine, it will by all means be proper to remove it; for there can be no comfort, living in perpetual fret and mifery, exclufive of the danger of the fuppreffion, and the repeated difagreeable circumftance of putting back the Stone with the catheter, which is fometimes attended, be the introduction ever fo expertly done, with an inflammation; befides the ill effects which the Urine kept in the Ureters and Pelvis of the Kidnies and veffels in the whole fyftem may have in the production of other fymptoms.

With thefe cautions, diets and medicines then we may keep ourfelves as eafy as our condition will admit; and we may comfort ourfelves with reflecting that we are not the only fufferers, if it be a fatiffaction to a generous mind that others are affected fo; for there are fome who curfe the gout, ferpigo, and the rheumatifm, for ending them no fooner; which fatality connected with our formation, being elegantly defcribed by the inimitable Mr. Grey, we fhall clofe this fection with his beautiful defcription of it.

> Lo, in the vale of years beneath
> A grifly troop are feen,
> The painful family of death,
> More hideous than their queen:

This

This racks the Joints, this fires the Veins,
That ev'ry labouring Sinew ſtrains,
   Thoſe in the deeper vitals rage :
Lo, Poverty, to fill the band,
That numbs the ſoul with icy hand,
   And ſlow-conſuming Age.

To each his ſufferings; all are Men,
   Condemn'd alike to groan ;
The tender for another's pain,
   Th' unfeeling for his own.
Yet ah! why ſhould they know their fate ?
Since Sorrow never comes too late,
   And happineſs too ſwiftly flies.
Thought would deſtroy their paradiſe.
No more; where ignorance is bliſs,
   'Tis folly to be wiſe.

F I N I S.

www.ingramcontent.com/pod-product-compliance
Lightning Source LLC
Chambersburg PA
CBHW020618030726
47497CB00007B/2310